Second Chance Christmas

Bindarra Creek Christmas in July Romance

Kerrie Paterson

The Writing Nook

Second Chance Christmas
Bindarra Creek Christmas in July Romance
By Kerrie Paterson

Copyright © Kerrie Paterson 2025

ISBN: 978-1-7640677-0-6

Ornament icon created by Nuricon - Flaticon.com
Cover design by Paradox Book Cover Design

Contents

Chapter One

S cott's large steel shed echoed with the buzz and hum of his welder. Fortunately for his neighbours, he'd positioned his shed far back on his acreage at Corella, a short drive west from Bindarra Creek.

He finished his final weld and reached over to turn off the welder. With a sigh of relief, he straightened and removed his helmet and ear-muffs. The sounds of the land rushed back in. One of his neighbours slashed his property, the tractor a distant hum. A cockatoo screeched as it flew overhead, the harsh sound a match for his welding.

Scott wiped his forehead with the back of his hand, reached for his water bottle and wandered outside. He rested his back against the shed wall. There wasn't much heat in the mid-autumn sun, but what warmth there was had soaked into the steel, soothing his aching back through his overalls. Eyes closed, he drank deeply.

Right about now, a big fat retirement fund would be nice, so he could kick back on the veranda with a beer, a book, and no plans beyond the next hour.

He snorted and pushed away from the wall. Like that would ever happen. He loved his work, but it would never make him rich. Sighing deeply, he walked back into the shed and leaned his hip against the tool bench, staring at his latest project with a critical eye. The fire pit would go brilliantly out at the Stars Cottages. Hopefully, with winter not far away, the guests could soon enjoy many nights around the campfire.

He'd used an old tractor rim as the fire pit base and welded discarded horseshoes together to form a unique rustic screen. Each set of five horseshoes created a star in the centre where they overlapped, the pattern repeating around the screen. He tilted his head, imagining how flames would flicker behind it, warming those who sat around the fire on cold, wintry nights. If Stevie and her guests liked it, he should add that design to his regular inventory.

Speaking of which... He picked up his phone and dialled a number.

"Hey, Stevie, Scott Gillespie here."

"Gilly, how's it going?" He smiled at the sound of Stevie's voice. It was sometimes hard to think of her as a middle-aged woman when he'd watched her grow up. She'd barely started school when he would work on her dad's farm as a fresh-faced apprentice, always wanting to tag along and pester him with questions. She'd quickly become a surrogate little sister.

"Good, thanks. Listen. I've finished that fire pit and, if I do say so myself, it's looking quite good. I've only got to tidy it up and then I'll bring it out. When suits?"

"You are fantastic! You're a legend, Gilly." He could hear the smile in her voice. "That's going to be such a draw card for our guests. Any time is fine. Just send me a text first. Luke's usually holed up in his study writing so he can give you a hand to get it off the truck if I'm not here."

"Awesome. Listen, I need to give it a final polish, and I'll probably bring it out on Tuesday?"

"Sounds great! I can't wait to see it. I should be around. Hey, are you going to the SES meeting this afternoon?"

"Yep, sure am." His heart gave an involuntary flutter at the thought.

"Cool. I'll see you there. Roman has some news that I'm sure you'll love."

Frowning, Scott hung up the phone and placed it back down on the tool bench. He wouldn't waste time thinking about Stevie's cryptic comment. He'd find out soon enough what the news was.

Before he finished Stevie's fire pit, he needed to jot down some ideas that had come to him while he was welding and in the zone. Dan at the Riverside Pub had asked him to create a sculpture to stand out the front as a memorial for Old Jake and he'd promised to get back with to him with some concepts soon. He spent a few minutes jotting down ideas that clamoured in his brain.

He checked his watch. Still a few hours to go until the State Emergency Service meeting. His stomach flipped. As much as he enjoyed seeing his mates in the crew, there was a bigger enticement for him. Ever since a certain redhead by the name Kimberley Ward had joined two years ago to help Roy with the paperwork, Scott's attendance had become much more regular.

He'd be fooling himself if he thought anything would come of it, either. She was way out of his league — too classy, too popular — but at least he could keep admiring her from afar.

Kimberley put down her shading pencil, linked her hands above her head, and stretched her back. It had taken hours, but finally she'd finished illustrating another page. She pushed her chair away from the desk and stepped back, looking at the drawing from a different angle.

She smiled, satisfied with the finished illustration. Like any creative project, she could keep tinkering with minor improvements, but she knew when enough was enough. In the drawing, a young girl sat on the lawn in front of an old country-style house, dolls and teddy bears surrounding her, a plastic tea set in the middle. She held a teacup to the mouth of the doll cradled in her arms, gazing down tenderly. A curious wombat peeked around the front picket fence and a mob of kangaroos stood alert in the paddock beside the house, their faces turned to watch the girl. High in the tree above the roos, the grey head of an owlet-nightjar was just visible in its hollow.

Tension drained out of Kimberley's shoulders, replaced with a warm glow of a job well done. She snapped a quick photo and fired it off to Jodie. Having a best friend who always badgered her for updates on her work was like having her own personal cheerleader.

Jodie sent back an emoji of a face with heart eyes. *Love it!*

Kimberley soaked up the positive feedback, even from her friend, a warm flush of validation spreading through her chest. Illustrating an entire book was like a solitary marathon, each completed page marking another kilometre conquered in isolation. Regular compliments kept her going.

Grinning, she gathered up all her crumpled test sketches and tossed them in the bin, dancing a happy dance as she aimed and shot. Two more pages to go and she could send the completed book off to her publisher.

As she bent to pick up a wayward ball of paper, her phone rang, Stevie's name flashing up on the screen.

"Hey, Stevie." Kimberley placed the phone on speaker while she packed her pencils back in their case. They had to go back in the right drawer and in order, otherwise she'd spend more time looking for the right shade than working.

"Did I catch you at a bad time? Are you still working?"

"All good. I've just finished for the day."

"Oh, that's great. What are you working on this time?"

Kimberley glanced back at her drawing, a grin stealing across her face again. "It's another kid's book, about a young girl who lives on a farm out in the bush with a plethora of cuddly Australian animals."

"Sounds cute! I can't wait to see it." A dog barked in the background of the call. "Lady, shh! Anyway, I rang to check if you're coming to the SES meeting this afternoon?"

Kimberley glanced at her watch. "I'll be there. I might be a bit late, though. It took me longer than expected to finish."

"It's not for a couple of hours. I only wanted to remind you. Apparently, the captain has some big news for us. The CWA ladies have come up with another plan that they want us to take part in. I rang to see if you had any inside knowledge."

Kimberley laughed. "Sorry, I haven't been to a meeting for ages. Roman didn't give any hints?"

"No." She could hear the pout in Stevie's voice. "He said we had to wait for tonight."

"Well, that will be something to look forward to. Anyway, I'd better get organised if I'm going to be there. I'll see you soon."

"I'll save you a seat. Bye."

While Kimberley had done her basic SES training, she mostly worked in the office. Maybe in the future she'd be confident enough to go out on calls. Confident enough to handle the chainsaws or climb ladders to fix roofs. Or knowledgeable enough to help on searches. She wanted to be a bigger part of the crew; she simply had to get over some of her fears first. Although if she was realistic, there was a greater chance of falls from ladders once a person was over fifty. Maybe she'd be better off sticking to what she was good at and staying in the office.

Kimberley strolled out to the kitchen and opened her freezer, looking for something quick and easy. She plucked a microwave meal at random. Fettuccine Carbonara. That would do. She shoved it in the microwave and hit the timer.

While that was cooking, she'd have time to check her email. She walked back into her office and opened her laptop, crossing her fingers as she clicked on her email icon. Hopefully, some news today. Even better, hopefully some good news. While the rational part of her brain wasn't expecting her book to make the short list of the children's book awards for the illustrations category, a part of her remained hopeful. The excitement of making the long list still buoyed her on the days when she felt like giving up and that nothing she drew was right. The microwave beeped from the kitchen as she refreshed her email and sighed. Still nothing. Was that a good or bad sign? Hopefully, whatever news the captain had today would take her mind off checking every hour.

She headed back to the kitchen and opened the microwave, avoiding the cloud of steam that floated out. Reaching for the meal, she winced as her fingers came in contact with the hot tray and tossed the meal quickly onto a plate.

At the sound of the microwave opening, her cat slunk into the kitchen, sat at her feet and meowed, begging for a share.

"Hey, Tibbles, I wondered where you were. You'll have to wait your turn. It's my lunchtime now."

Tibbles sent her an indignant glare and stalked over to sit next to his food bowl, eyes fixed firmly on her. She sighed. She knew how this would end. If she wanted to eat in peace, she'd need to feed him first. Otherwise, she'd have to endure his glare and howls until she gave in.

"How was your day? Mine was fine. Thank you for asking." She reached into the cupboard for his kibble and poured it into the bowl.

As soon as Tibbles heard the metallic clink of the first kibble hitting the bowl, he stuck his head under the stream and began eating as if he hadn't eaten for three days.

"Great conversationalist, you are. It's not that you're not good company, Tibbles, but it would be nice to talk to another human over a meal occasionally."

She sighed, washed her hands and went back to her lonely meal for one.

Scott hurried up the steps to the SES headquarters, his footsteps echoing on the wooden treads, and pushed open the door. He was running late, and the mostly occupied chairs suggested the meeting was close to starting. Nodding a quick greeting to Nancy and Bob, he slipped into a chair at the back of the rows. His gaze zeroed in on the flash of red hair. He couldn't help himself. She drew him like a magnet.

There she was. Kimberley was setting a cup of tea in front of Roy, smiling and patting him on the shoulder. At ninety-five, Roy Towns deserved all the pampering he could get. Kimberley had been a godsend, helping him out with the paperwork and administration tasks that were beyond him now. She had that effortless charm that drew everyone to her. Everyone liked her. Everyone wanted a word and a smile. And she barely knew he existed.

He wracked his brain for an excuse to talk to her after the meeting. His first aid certificate was due for renewal soon — maybe he could ask her about the next training dates?

"All right. Everyone settle down." Roman stepped up to the front of the room and gave his best impression of a serious glare. Conversations dwindled off and chair legs scraped on the wooden floor as everyone turned their attention to the captain.

"Alrighty. First thing on the agenda today." He looked up from his notes and grinned. "I'm sure you've all heard about Edwina Lette's latest ambitious plan?"

"You mean her Christmas in July thing. Isn't one Christmas enough? Do we have to have it twice?"

Scott couldn't see who had called out, but the man's quip earned him a few chuckles. He laughed too, but deep down he knew, like most of them did, that the town would be in dire straits if it wasn't for the efforts of Edwina and all her Country Women's Association cronies. The woman was unstoppable.

Not that he was a fan of one Christmas a year, let alone two. Although none could be worse than the one when he'd woken up to an empty house and a 'Dear John' note on the kitchen table.

Roman nodded and looked down at his notes again. "That's the one. She's got all manner of things planned. I know her list includes carols, a parade, bonfire night with food stalls. I'm sure there's a lot more on the agenda."

"Does she want us to help with setting up road barriers, collecting donations? All the usual? Probably cooking up the barbie as well?" Roy's voice quavered as he asked what they were all thinking.

"I imagine she will. I haven't been told all the details yet, but I assume she'll rely on us like she usually does for the manual labour."

Leslie flexed his muscles, well-developed from his hours in the gym. "Well, that's what we're best at." The crew snorted.

"As I was about to say, they haven't given us exact details yet, but there is one thing she was adamant about — she wanted the SES to enter a float in the parade."

"A float? You've got to be kidding me! Like Mardi Gras?"

"Well, you can dress up in sparkles and glitter if you like, Leslie, but I think she wants it more Christmas-themed." Scott snorted at the thought of the stout, muscle-bound guy wearing sparkles. Maybe he could sprinkle the glitter on his bushy ginger beard.

Roman raised his voice above the laughter and good-natured banter. "Do we have any volunteers to work on it? I'm afraid I'm out, sorry. I'm up to my eyeballs in reno work and the kids at the moment."

The room was silent. A tap dripped somewhere in the building, echoing in the hush. Kimberley raised a tentative hand. "I'm happy to help if I can."

Scott's heart leapt, and he almost sat on his hand to stop himself from volunteering. If he jumped in immediately, everyone would know that all he wanted was to spend time with Kimberley.

Stevie raised her hand. "I reckon Gilly would be a good one to help. Between him and Kimberley, I think you've got a fair bit of Bindarra Creek's artistic talent. Apart from you, of course, Roman, but you've already ruled yourself out."

In unison, all eyes turned to Scott. He shrugged and nodded. "Sure, I have time to help with that." Had he pulled off an air of nonchalance? His cheeks warmed, and he hunched down further in his seat.

"Okay thanks, guys. Can you two get together and come up with some plans to run past us? Maybe email your initial plans and everyone can have their say."

Kimberley glanced at Scott for confirmation and nodded. "No worries, we can do that."

All Scott could think about for the rest of the meeting was the torture of working with Kimberley. Roman could have announced that they were driving the rescue boat down the main street, and he wouldn't have even blinked. Hopefully, someone would catch him up if he missed anything important.

He came to his senses as everyone stood and began chatting again. Obviously, the meeting was over. He glanced up and there she was in front of him; her smile lighting up her face.

"This feels like a class project. Guess we're working together?"

Heart pounding, he forced himself to smile back. "I guess. When do you want to get together and talk through some ideas?" He tried not to sound too eager. Her social calendar was likely very full, unlike his own. Other than SES training and his work commitments, his schedule was pathetically empty.

"I'm free whenever over the next week."

Scott blinked. That was unexpected. "How about Monday morning at the cafe?"

"Sure, that suits me. 10ish?"

"Perfect. I'll be ready for another coffee by then. I'll see you there."

He drove home in a daze, already counting down the hours until he saw her again.

Chapter Two

K imberley paused in the doorway to the cafe and looked around, wondering if Scott was there already. Small groups of mums with pre-school aged kids and babies filled the booths along the far wall, likely seeking shelter from the chilly wind outside. Elderly couples sat at the freestanding tables, steaming beverages and sweet treats in front of them. She waved to a few familiar faces. Maybe the couples she didn't know were grey nomads on their way north for the winter. In a couple of months, when winter was at its peak, she'd undoubtedly wish she could join them. She finally spotted Scott in the far corner and made her way over. He looked up from his phone as she neared, and half stood while she pulled out the chair opposite.

"Hi." She unwound her scarf from her neck, shrugged out of her coat and draped them both over the back of the chair. Sinking into her seat, she rubbed her hands together to warm them.

"Hi to you too. Should we order first and then chat about the float?" She leaned forward to hear him better over the laughter and chatter of the other patrons, punctuated by the occasional squeal from the kids.

"That sounds like an excellent idea. It smells so amazing in here that I won't be able to concentrate unless I eat." Kimberley swivelled to read the blackboard menu near the till and immediately pivoted back. "I don't know why I even bothered to look at the menu. I always have the same thing."

"And what's your regular order?"

"A latte and I can never go past Thea's baklava." Thoughts of the honey and cinnamon pastry made her mouth water in anticipation.

Scott stood, pushing his chair back. "I'll go up and order. Can I get you anything else?"

"Thank you." She reached down for her handbag. "I'll give you the cash for mine."

He waved a hand to dismiss her offer. "Don't worry about it. I'm happy to pay."

"Oh! If you're sure." She wasn't sure of the protocol here. Usually, she split the bill with her friends, so Scott's offer was unexpected. "Thanks. I'll owe you one."

He ducked his head and smiled, then walked over to the counter.

Kimberley took the time to study Scott while he waited in line. She'd known him as part of the SES since she started. He was quiet, reserved and always willing to lend a hand, but that was about all she knew about him. She'd never spent one-on-one time with him. Somehow, when she'd worked on SES projects, she'd always paired up with other members of the crew.

Tall and solidly built, the width of his shoulders was emphasised by the knitted jumper he wore. His beard was trim, its black peppered liberally with grey. He glanced over as he reached the counter, catching her gaze on him, and gave a half-smile.

The tips of her ears burned that he'd caught her staring. People-watching came as second nature to her, studying facial expressions and body language to capture in her drawing. Was that honestly why she'd been studying Scott, though? Or was she enjoying the view of an attractive man? She busied herself straightening the salt and pepper pots on the table. He sat back down at the table, and she raised her head, cheeks warm.

"Orders will be here soon." He laced his fingers together, leaned his elbows on the table and cleared his throat. "Christmas in July, huh? Are you a Christmas fan?"

Kimberley grinned. "You have no idea how much of a Christmas fan I am. I love it. I'm like a big kid in December." Truth be told, her feelings were more complex than that, but it was mostly true. "I've never had a Christmas in July town event, though, so this will certainly be a novelty. It will be nice to have a cold Christmas. Possibly even a white Christmas."

Why was she rambling? What was it about Scott's warm gaze that made her so flustered? She drew in an unsteady breath, trying to fill her tight chest with oxygen. "You look a little pained. I'm guessing you're not a Christmas fan?"

Scott grimaced and made a seesaw motion with his hand. "Not a huge fan, to be honest. I have a few bad memories from Christmas past. Plus, I find as an adult there's not too much to get excited about. Not when I don't have kids. Sorry, I sound like Scrooge."

"Not at all. I think many adults are like that." Some Christmases even she had to make an effort to get into the spirit and keep her vow to celebrate the event.

He sat back in his chair and stroked his beard. "Enough about me. Where are you from originally? I know you've only been here in Bindarra Creek for a couple of years."

"It's coming up on three years now. I'm originally from Sydney." The time had gone so quickly. Her life in the city seemed like another lifetime.

Scott's face stilled. "That's quite a change!"

"I wanted a new start after my divorce. And the houses out here were so much more affordable than in Sydney. I heard about this place on the radio when they had one of their other events. Anyway, it seemed like a nice place to come and here I am."

A frown flickered across his brow. "You don't miss Sydney?"

"I do sometimes. Bindarra Creek is a slower lifestyle, that's for sure. But I like it." It had been an adjustment at the start, but now she'd fully embraced life in the small town.

They sat back while Nick placed their order on the table. They exchanged a quick greeting before he hurried off to deal with the next order.

Kimberley forked up a bite of her baklava, the flavours exploding on her tastebuds. "What about you? Have you lived in Bindarra Creek for long?"

"In and around the area all my life." Scott lifted his mug to his lips, the rich, sweet aroma of his Greek coffee filling the air.

She'd never been brave enough to try it, but she'd been told the thick brew was an acquired taste. "You've never wanted to leave?"

"Nah, I like it here. Good people. They've got your back. And my family's around here so. I couldn't see much point heading off to the Big Smoke."

"That makes sense." Kimberley took a sip of her latte and licked the foam off her top lip. "I guess we need to talk about the float. Any ideas?"

"Well, according to Roman, it needs to be Christmas-themed, and maybe we can work the SES into it somehow?" He chuckled. "An abseiling Santa or something?"

She laughed as the image formed in her mind. "That's a fabulous idea. I can see that on the back of a truck. Stevie mentioned you're artistic. What's your special skills?"

Scott shuffled in his seat and stared down into his coffee. "I'm a welder by trade. But I do metal sculptures as well."

"Oh, that sounds perfect. Could you weld something like an abseiling A-frame?" She stirred her coffee, then tapped the spoon against her upper lip while she thought. "I guess we can't have it too high, though. If it's like last Christmas, the committee will string tinsel strands across the Main St. We don't want to wipe out all of Edwina's decorations as we pass by in our float."

Scott laughed, a deep rumble that crinkled the corners of his eyes. "I can picture that. Our truck dragging behind all the tinsel and garlands. And Edwina running after us, pitching a pink fit."

The image was so absurd that Kimberley couldn't help giggling. "Honestly, that could be worth it." It was a pleasant surprise to discover Scott had an amazing sense of humour. "Okay, so we have an abseiling Santa. I'm a children's book illustrator. Could we have Australian animals around the base looking up at him? Maybe wearing Christmas hats? I could paint those."

She picked up her phone, flicked through her photo gallery, and held it out for Scott to see. "This is my latest book that was published last year, about endangered species. I could draw something like these?"

Scott leaned forward to look at the screen more closely. "Cool. I'm pretty sure my nephew's kids have got this book. I remember reading it to them. The illustrations are amazing — so detailed."

Her cheeks flushed with warmth at the unexpected compliment. "Thanks. It's actually been long listed for a children's book award." She hadn't meant to tell anyone other than her close friends, but the words burst out of her.

"Well done you. That's fantastic." He lifted his coffee cup in a salute. "You must be excited."

"I am. I'm not sure when the shortlist nominations come out, but I keep checking my email in case. The chances are pretty low, but even so, it's something to add to my bio."

"Seriously, you should be proud. These are awesome."

"Thanks." She tucked her phone back into her bag. "Do you think we need to come up with more ideas or will that be enough for Roman?"

Scott grinned. "To be honest, I don't think Roman would care. I think he has enough on his plate. One should be enough. And it's a killer idea, I think."

Scott had to almost kick himself that he was sitting opposite Kimberley, laughing with her, sharing a meal. Who would have thought that a Christmas float would force him into a scenario he'd only dreamt of? And it was going to be over too quickly. They'd finalised their ideas for the float, and only crumbs remained on their plates. He searched for a way to prolong the meeting.

"Did you study to be an artist?"

Kimberley nodded and named a prestigious art school in Sydney. "I was lucky enough to get a scholarship."

"Wow, that's impressive." He was self-taught, lacking any formal art education.

"It's been many years of odd jobs before I could make a living as a children's book illustrator, though. I worked in marketing, hospitality — lots of random jobs totally unrelated to art. Heck, I was even a children's face painter for a while, doing parties and events. I'm quite lucky now that I'm making a living doing something I love."

"I'd say a combination of hard work and talent."

She screwed up her face. "And a lot of luck! What about you? How did you get into metal sculpture?"

"At school, I loved art and metalwork. I was a hands-on learner, not a textbook kid. I got a welding apprenticeship when I left in Year 10. I was keen to leave school and do something practical. While I was practising, I used to muck around with welding up scrap metal, spare nuts and bolts and so on. Then I started creating these character sculptures that took on a life of their own, and it grew from there."

"That's fascinating." The way she gazed at him, like she was really listening, made him think she was genuine in her praise. "Do you have any photos of what you've done?"

Scott reached for his phone and pulled up his website. He navigated to the gallery and handed it over to Kimberley.

She took the phone and scrolled, her eyes lighting up. "These are so clever." Eyes shining, she glanced up at him. "I think I've seen some of your sculptures around town, but didn't realise you'd made them. And you sell these little characters in the gift shop, don't you?"

He nodded, warmth spreading in his chest that she'd taken notice of his sculptures and that she liked them. They were whimsical little things: characters made from nuts and bolts, dragons made from horseshoes, and his cut-out metal bird silhouettes.

"You seem to do a lot of birds."

"I do, yeah. I wouldn't say I specialise in them, but I do an awful lot, especially magpies. Noisy blighters, but I like their song."

Kimberley laughed. "Vicious at springtime, though."

He rubbed his head, almost feeling the pain of their sharp beak on his scalp as they attacked to protect their young. "For sure, and I've got the scars to prove it."

She leaned forward as if she was going to impart the secrets of the world. "I actually have a bird character that I hide in as many illustrations as I can get away with."

"Really?" He cast his mind back over the book he'd read, trying to think if he'd spotted it.

"Yes, he's a little owlet-nightjar. I call him Scrappy, and I try to hide him in all my scenes. I don't always get away with it, but if you look carefully, he's in most of them."

"I'll have to check out your books more closely." He hesitated. "Are you into bird watching?" He almost smacked his forehead with how lame that sounded. Not everyone was as geeky as him. While he wouldn't call himself a twitcher, he enjoyed going out to watch them and get inspiration for his work.

"Maybe not bird watching, per se, but I love taking my camera out and trying to get good reference photos." She took a final look at his website and handed him back his phone. "Have you got any special places?"

"I sure do." In for a penny, in for a pound. He'd already proven his geekiness. "Would you like to come with me one day?"

Her eyes lit up. "I'd love that. Thank you."

"I'm a bit of an early bird ..." He chuckled. "No pun intended, so I like to go out at dawn. But I know not everyone's like that. We could do whatever time suits you."

"I think I'm becoming more of an early bird as I get older." She rested her chin on her hand and gazed toward the back of the café, her expression pensive. "I don't sleep as much, and I definitely can't do anything too late at night without major repercussions the next day."

He laughed. "I feel you there. I used to go out to B&S balls, party all night, catch a couple of hours of sleep in the back of the ute and rock up to work the next day, bright-eyed and bushy tailed." He shook his head with a grin, memories of wild nights flashing through his mind. "No way I could do that now. I won't even start a movie after 7pm."

She chuckled. "Getting old is a dreadful thing, isn't it?"

"Yes, but better than the alternative." He sobered as he thought about a couple of his mates who didn't have the privilege of growing old, lost to accident, mental health, or illness.

For a moment, she was silent too, lost in her own thoughts.

He grimaced. "Sorry, I've brought the mood down there."

A faint smile pulled at her mouth as she glanced at her watch. "No, that's okay. Just lost in my own melancholy thoughts." She drained the last of her latte and placed the mug back down on the table with a clunk. "I should get going. Do you want me to email the crew with the idea that we came up with?"

He kicked himself for bringing an end to their conversation with his flippant remark. "Yes, please. At least that way we can start to make plans — what material we need, what time we both have and so on?"

She stood and shrugged into her jacket. "Sounds good. I'll be in touch once we get the go ahead from everyone, and we can decide on next steps." She smiled, dazzling him. "I'm really looking forward to working with you on this. It should be fun."

"Me too. I can't wait."

She dashed out of the cafe, leaving him to wonder what he'd done to scare her off.

Chapter Three

The following morning, Kimberley was still beating herself up for rushing out of the cafe the way she had. She'd been having a great time until her thoughts had veered into gloomy territory, and she'd thought about the one she'd lost. He would have been forty this year, possibly with kids of his own. And now he'd never get the chance.

That was why she celebrated Christmas so hard, celebrating it for her darling Toby and all the others who couldn't, who were no longer there to celebrate.

Shaking her head to clear it of the melancholy thoughts, she sat down at the computer. She didn't normally let the memories get her down, even at Christmas, which was the hardest time. It wasn't clear what had triggered the depressing thoughts this time, but she'd had to leave the cafe as soon as possible.

She brought up her email program and typed out a quick email to the SES crew. Her lips curved into a smile as she outlined the plans they had come up with, her body tingling with creative energy. Having seen Scott's art, she couldn't wait to see what they could create together.

Tibbles jumped onto the desk and stopped with his foot hovering over the keyboard. "No!" Her warning was pointless. He glared at her and then tap-danced right across the keyboard.

"Tibbles!" She picked him up, gave him a quick cuddle, and dropped him gently on the floor beside her. He sent her a disdainful glare, plopped down and washed himself.

Kimberley rolled her eyes and laughed, then looked back at the jumbled mess of email. She removed Tibbles' contribution, re-read it and hit send. Done. Hopefully everyone liked their ideas.

Pushing her chair back to stand, she disturbed the cat, receiving yet another glare.

"You're such an ungrateful creature. I don't know why I put up with you." She stooped to scratch his head before wandering into the kitchen. Grabbing pen and paper, she opened her pantry to put together a shopping list. Pasta, tin tomatoes, chocolate. What else?

She'd enjoyed chatting with Scott yesterday. While she'd always thought of him as quiet, she'd now classify him as reserved rather than shy. He'd lit up when they'd discussed art, his eyes shining with enthusiasm. Finding someone else so passionate about their creativity thrilled her. Sure, she had plenty of friends in Bindarra Creek, but she hadn't made any artistic friends. Someone who felt that same drive to create, to express themselves through their art. She'd felt a connection with Scott. Could they develop a friendship beyond the float project?

Curiosity got the best of her. She picked up her phone, opened her social media app and typed in Scott's name, scrolling through the suggestions until she found what looked like his account. The profile image showed a group of men in bright orange SES overalls, and while it was too small to see faces clearly, it looked like their headquarters behind them.

She clicked on the profile, scrolling through the few photos that were public. Several photos of landscapes around the area, one of him and another man. Brother, friend or partner? There were no photos of anyone who looked like they might be a wife or girlfriend.

For a long minute, her finger hovered over the Add Friend button. Would he think it was weird? She wouldn't take it personally if he didn't respond. Maybe he didn't even use social media. She wasn't a big user herself, tending to mostly scroll rather than post. Adding him as a friend wasn't inappropriate — she was friends on the app with many of the SES crew and CWA members. Heart thumping, she pressed the button. *Friend request sent.*

Forcing herself to put down the phone, she grabbed her keys and bag and walked to the IGA supermarket. As she wandered the aisles, her phone pinged several times with email notifications as replies to her email trickled in from the crew. Whenever the notification ping sound rang out, her heart leapt. Had Scott responded to her social media friend request?

And each time her emotions nose-dived when she opened the notification to see another email from crew members. Was she so starved for connection that she was desperate for him to accept?

Stevie: *Sounds awesome. The kids will love it!*

Roman: *Can't wait to see this. And Edwina's reaction!*

She pushed her phone to the bottom of her bag and forced herself to finish her shopping. Luckily, there weren't many other customers, and it didn't take long to grab the few items she needed.

"Hi, Nancy." She smiled at the IGA owner as she transferred her items from the shopping basket to the counter.

"Hello, Kimberley, dear." Nancy grabbed the first item to ring up, holding up the packet of dried spaghetti. "You should go along to the Italian cooking class — I think it starts next week. Fresh pasta is better than this, so they tell me. Or there are class in Greek cooking, Nepalese, Scottish and what was the other one?" She was silent for a minute as she placed the pasta in Kimberley's shopping bag. "Oh, Japanese. That's right. Maki Fukuka's running that one."

Kimberley laughed. "They sound fun, but cooking isn't my strength at all. I'll stick with the basics."

"I was tempted to send Bob along. The man can barely make a sandwich without help." She read the total out to Kimberley and waited for her to tap her card. "Here's your receipt. Have a lovely day, dear."

"You, too." Kimberley hefted her bags and left the supermarket. She needed to go home and start work for the day but couldn't resist detouring past the gift shop on her way.

As she stepped in, a young man behind the counter greeted her. "Good morning. Can I help you?"

"Just having a quick look, thanks. I've got my cousin's birthday coming up, so I thought I'd check out what you've got in that's new."

If anything caught her eye for her cousin's birthday, she might buy it, but she had to admit to herself that it wasn't the main reason she was there. She was there to examine to Scott's sculptures. The nuts-and-bolts creations had made her laugh before, but now she stood and scrutinised them, acknowledging the talent in creating quirky characters out of such mundane objects. They showed such personality — the man leaning back against a tree, fishing rod in hand, hat pulled over his eyes, the group of kids playing tag with a small puppy, the woman hanging her clothes on an old-fashioned clothesline.

How did he create such character with only a few nuts and bolts?

She stepped back to look up at his metal sculptures hanging on the wall. Rusted metal birds of various breeds: a cockatoo in full flight, an emu staring her in the eyes and, of course, a magpie with his head flung back. She could almost hear the joyous warble coming from his throat.

She would come back and buy one of these for her cousin, but she was also going to buy one for herself. She felt like a schoolgirl with a crush.

Her phone pinged again, and she tapped the screen to bring it to life. *Scott Gillespie has accepted your friend request.*

A grin spread over her face. What was she? Sixteen? Tingles and shivers ran through her body when she thought about the fact that very soon, she'd be spending hours working closely with him. But it wasn't simply the prospect of being near him that made her heart race, it was the opportunity to explore the rapport she hoped was mutual.

What would it be like to hear him talk about his process? To watch those hands that crafted such unique creations move as he explained where his inspirations came from? She imagined late afternoon conversations over coffee, discussing where their ideas came from and how they brought them to life from that initial spark of creativity.

She wanted to know what made Scott Gillespie tick when no one was watching. What books shaped him? What music moved him? What fears kept him up at night? The possibility of that connection, of truly seeing someone and being seen in return... that was what sent electricity dancing across her skin at the thought of working with him.

On Tuesday afternoon, Scott pulled his truck to a halt in Stevie's driveway, switched off the engine, and jumped down from the cab. The screen door slammed shut and Stevie hurried down the back steps. She came to a halt beside him and reached up to give him a hug.

"I can't wait to see this!" She craned her neck as if she could see under the tarp.

"Patience, grasshopper." He ruffled her hair like he used to when she was little. It had the desired effect of annoying her as much now as it did then.

She shuffled from foot to foot. "Come on!"

Scott rolled his eyes. "How about you show me where you want it first before I uncover it?"

"Fine." Already heading off toward the cottages, she called back over her shoulder, "Keep up, old man!" She came to a standstill in a clearing at the front of the two small holiday cabins. "I thought we could put it around here. That way guests from either of the cottages can use it, or we can have combined campfires easily. I'm so excited!"

Scott inspected the area and found a flat spot that was suitably cleared. He stamped on the area to mark the grass. "What about here?"

Stevie eyed the distance from the cottages. "Looks pretty perfect. We can add some seating out here later, maybe some hay bales for the authentic experience or we can go upmarket with outdoor furniture."

"Okay, you stand here on this spot, and I'll back the truck up."

"Are you going to use me as target practice?"

He raised an eyebrow and grinned. "Don't tempt me, Stevie."

She laughed and walked over to the spot, taking her place as he left. "Just remember I'm little. I feel like I need a flag so that you can see me."

"Just yell loudly. I know you're capable of that." Still grinning, he walked back to his truck and reversed it alongside where Stevie stood. He leapt up onto the back of the truck and undid the ropes holding down the tarp.

Stevie raised herself on tiptoes. "Can I see it yet?"

"Just about. Hop out of the way now." He tossed the tarp to the side, hooked the firepit to the small crane on the back of the truck and lowered it into the spot they'd designated.

"I love it!" Stevie walked around, inspecting it from all sides. "Oh! The horseshoes make a star shape — perfect for Stars Cottages. You are so talented, Gilly. Thanks, mate."

"The invoice is in the mail, squirt. Don't go thinking it was a freebie."

Stevie cocked her head to the side and raised an eyebrow. "Speaking of talented, how did your meeting go with the lovely Kimberley yesterday? I heard rumours you two were looking very cosy at the Cyprus Café."

"I wouldn't call it cosy." He tipped his head to one side as he thought about sitting opposite her in the café. "Kimberley is easy to talk to. We have a lot in common, so we had plenty to talk about. And she had some great ideas for the float." He remembered the way her eyes had sparkled as she'd talked about her work. The way her mouth lifted into a ready smile that could lighten any sombre mood. "I think we'll work well together on this project."

"It could be the start of something beautiful." Her cheeky grin blossomed.

He narrowed his eyes. "Don't go getting any ideas, Stephanie Ryan."

She widened her eyes innocently. "Who, me?"

"Yes, you. No grand matchmaking plans, okay? We're simply two people working on a project together. I'm not ready to rush into anything. After the mess I made of my marriage, I need to be careful this time. There's the potential for us to be good friends. We bonded over our creativity, and the last thing I want to do is stuff that up."

"You keep thinking that, Gilly," Stevie teased. "We'll see."

Scott shook his head and smiled. He'd admired Kimberley from afar for so long, he was happy to keep their relationship in the friend zone before making any long-term commitments.

Chapter Four

On Sunday morning, Kimberley drove out to Scott's house for their first detailed planning session. Her tyres rattled over Swallows Bridge as she crossed the creek, swollen from recent heavy rain. The road meandered past new housing developments and tree-lined paddocks, dipping through hollows before revealing smaller acreages nestled in the countryside.

Slowing down, she checked the street numbers against Scott's address scribbled on the note in her. When she spotted his place, she flicked on her turn signal, then drove down his driveway, the large metal gates open in welcome.

She parked near the small single-storey pale yellow weatherboard house and stepped out of the car. The air smelled fresh, with a hint of rose from the bushes bordering the front steps. She stood motionless for a moment, admiring the view. Rows of posts and wire covered a nearby property, bare grape vines twined over them with a few remaining leaves clinging tight. A hill beyond that broke the horizon, its green foliage a contrast to the dull grey sky.

Between the house and the two big steel sheds at the back of the property, sculptures dotted the yard, far bigger than any of his works that she'd seen before. A life-size swaggy with his possessions flung over his back, cut out in rusted metal, a rearing horse made from what looked like old car parts. He was incredibly talented. But where was he?

Metal clanged from one of the sheds. That answered her question. A delicious tremor raced up Kimberley's spine as she realised she was moments away from seeing not only Scott, but hopefully the inner sanctum where his art came to life.

What would Scott's creative space reveal? From his sculptures, she expected something both organised and imaginative — perhaps tools arranged with precision alongside piles of random materials and half-finished projects. With its combination of structure and unique elements, his art suggested a mind that valued both order and creative freedom.

The wide shed door stood open, and she strolled toward the rhythmic clang of a hammer striking steel. She hesitated at the entrance, banging her knuckles on the metal door to be heard over the sound. While she waited for him to notice her, she couldn't resist a peek around the workspace. Expansive windows flooded the interior with light even on such a dull day. A long workbench stretched along one side and across the rear of the shed, with a set of shelves above it holding organiser drawers and paint tins. Welding equipment stood beside a platform where the beginning of a sculpture took place, though what it might become was a mystery to her.

Scott laid down his hammer, straightened and took off his earmuffs. "Hi." He gave a shy smile. "You found the place all right?"

"I did. I can't believe I've lived here for three years and haven't been out to the Corella area before, though."

He grinned. "Well, there's not a lot out here, only some houses and a few shops. It's somewhere you really need to have a reason to visit."

He stepped down from the platform. "Please come in. It's nothing fancy but have a look around."

"Was it that obvious that I wanted to check it out?" Not needing a second invitation, she stepped inside the workshop.

He let out a deep laugh as he walked over to the workbench and placed his hammer down. "I'm the same. I love seeing where other people create."

As she'd expected, his workshop was meticulous, every item having its own place. A large pegboard stretched above the workbenches, tools hanging from hooks, each surrounded by a white outline marking its absence when in use. Order was something she deeply admired. Like him, she couldn't create in chaos either.

She stepped closer to the workbench, closer to Scott. A metallic smell in the air mingled with his spicy scent. Her nerves fluttered. "What are you working on?"

Reaching up, he tapped a sketch pinned on the pegboard above him. "Armidale Council wants a magpie sculpture for one of their parks."

Even though his sketches were rudimentary, she could envision the finished design, as if the magpie was about to cock its head and give her an inquisitive look. "That's amazing. You'll have to let me know when it's finished so I can see the finished product *in situ*."

His cheeks coloured. "Sure, if you're interested."

As she leaned forward to look at another sketch, her shoulder brushed against his. "What's this one?"

He froze for a minute, then straightened a wrench on the pegboard. "I've been playing with some ideas for a commission for Dan at the Riverside Pub. Do you remember Old Man Jake?"

"He was the caretaker at the pub, right? The old guy with his cockatoo on his shoulder." She pointed at the sketch. "I can tell it's him from the silhouette."

Scott smiled a little sadly. "That was him. Dan wants to put a sculpture out the front and asked me to show him a few ideas. I'm still in the concept stage though. Not ready to share anything with him yet."

He turned away and pointed his thumb toward the open door. "Come on. I'll show you the truck we'll use for the parade float, and then we can grab a cuppa and talk out some more ideas for the design."

"Sounds like a plan." Kimberley patted her satchel slung over her shoulder. "I bought some sketch pads so we can start drawing out the ideas."

"Perfect. The truck's in the other shed." He reached into his pocket and pulled out a bunch of keys.

She followed him toward the other shed, tucked behind his workshop. For a few minutes, he wrestled with the large padlock before flinging the door open with a screech that echoed around the area.

Grinning, Kimberley glanced around at the peaceful neighbourhood. "You're lucky to not have many neighbours."

Scott nodded. "Yep, that's why I moved out here, so that I could make as much noise as I wanted without disturbing people — within reason, of course." He smiled and waved his hand towards the darkened interior of the shed. "After you."

She stepped inside and waited for a moment for her eyes to adjust to the gloom. He reached beside her and fumbled with something on the wall. A minute later, bright light flooded the space to reveal an old, restored flatbed truck, its red paint gleaming in the lights.

"Oh, wow. I don't know much about old vehicles, but it's gorgeous. Did you restore it?"

"Yeah, me and my brother. My dad started us off, and when he passed away, we finished it as a bit of a tribute to him." He picked up the cloth draped over the side mirror and flicked a cobweb from the front headlight. She wasn't sure how long it had been since his father had passed away, but Scott's grief still showed in his bowed shoulders.

"I'm sure he would have loved it." Eager to give him some privacy, she walked to the back of the vehicle, examining the expanse of the flatbed.

A few minutes later, he joined her. "What do you think? Will it be suitable for the parade?"

"Are you sure you want to use it? It obviously means a great deal to you."

His face softened. "I take it out on special occasions. Its registration classifies it as a historic vehicle, so I can't take it out too often, but we've driven it in parades and Anzac Day marches and whatever else Edwina comes up with."

"In that case, I think it will be perfect." She walked to the side, considering how much space was available on the back of the truck. "How do you think should we set it out?"

Scott stepped up beside her and waved a hand towards the front of the tray. "I thought we could have the abseiling frame here at the front. That will leave room at the back for whichever lucky people get to ride on the float this year."

Kimberley grinned wryly. "You mean the same lucky people who were nominated to put the float together?"

He barked out a laugh. "More than likely. And it's good of you to go along with it."

"I'm looking forward to it. We're going to make the best float in the parade together." She glanced up to see his gaze on her. Their glances collided, and for a moment, time seemed to suspend between them.

"I'm looking forward to it, too." The answering light in his eyes made her heart skip a beat.

Their connection lingered in a mutual, silent agreement neither of them could guarantee an outcome on. A collaboration that could lead to a friendship. Maybe something more, maybe nothing at all.

A stray gust of wind blew the door shut, the bang echoing around the shed. Scott blinked and looked away. "I'll take some measurements, if you'd like to write them down, and then we'll head back to the house for a cuppa and see where we're at."

Pulse racing, she reached into her satchel for a notebook and pen. Her hands shook from the charged moment, making it difficult for her to turn to a blank page.

Scott pulled a tape measure from his pocket and leapt lightly onto the back of the truck. *Good grief.* She wished she had that mobility.

"Can you hold the end there? Thanks." She positioned the end of the tape measure where he indicated, holding it steady as he walked backward toward the truck's end. After jotting down the length measurement he called out, they repeated the process for the width, their silent coordination creating an efficient rhythm between them.

"That should be all we need." He tucked the tape measure back in his pocket. "The only thing we need to worry about with the height is not to take out the Christmas decorations."

She snickered at his reminder of their conversation in the café. "Yes, we don't want to be banned from every future Bindarra Creek parade."

He leapt down from the truck and landed beside her. "Right, now for the fun part."

Scott held the door open for Kimberley to proceed him into the house. His back door led straight into the kitchen, and even though he'd done a hurried clean, he checked to make sure there was nothing out of place. He wasn't a slob by any means, but living on his own, he didn't bother tidying as often as he probably should.

She stepped to the side, her eyes resting on his coffee machine. "Wow, you take your coffee seriously."

He patted the gleaming machine. It had cost him an amount he'd never admit to, but it had been his reward when he'd first received an interstate commission. "I sure do. It's an art form. You can add barista to the list of odd jobs I've done to make ends meet."

Kimberley frowned, eyeing the machine as if it might bite. "I've never done that one. You'll have to teach me the finer points."

"Uh, sure. What would you like me to make for you now?" He rubbed the back of his neck. While he'd made coffee for many people, his urge to impress her was overwhelming.

She pursed her lips and tapped her finger against them as she thought. "Can you do the fancy foam art on the top of the coffee?"

He winced and waggled his hand back and forth in a so-so gesture. "It's a skill I'm still practising, but happy to show you what I can do."

"All right, I'll have a latte with foam art." She placed her satchel down on the kitchen table. "Can I do anything to help?"

"No, you can stand here and watch the master at work." Scott couldn't believe he was standing in his kitchen with Kimberley, bantering as if they'd been friends for years. "Take a seat while I make it."

"I love your table." She ran a hand over the rustic wooden slab that formed his tabletop as she sank into a seat. "Did you make it?"

"I wish. No, my forte is metalwork, not wood. I bought it from a local who makes them."

"My kitchen is still a daggy 70s style from the last owners. Avocado green counters and burnt orange linos. It's not something you want to look at with a migraine." She laughed. "One day, I'll have the savings to fix it up."

"It sounds … something, that's for sure." He reached up into the cupboard for the coffee beans and measured them into the grinder. For a few minutes, conversation was impossible while the grinder whined, the machine rumbled, steam hissed and spat. He could feel her eyes on him, watching each step and forced himself to concentrate. The last thing he wanted was to burn himself like a rookie.

Finally, he produced a not perfect, but passable latte adorned with a foam heart and slid it onto the table in front of her. She examined it, then looked at him with a twinkle in her eye. "I'd hire you. If I owned a cafe, of course."

He laughed. "Is that in the foreseeable future?"

She screwed up her face and considered. "Not at all. I wouldn't want to go into competition against Thea's café, anyway."

He cleaned the machine with practiced efficiency and quickly prepared his own black coffee. Steam rose from his mug as he picked it up. "The house is still a little bit chilly. I had the fire going last night, but it died down somewhere in the early hours." He ran a hand over his beard. "Would you like to take our coffees outside? I've got a pergola around the side that catches the sun at this time of day."

"Sure." She stood, slung her bag over shoulder and picked up her coffee.

He led the way around to the covered area, placed his coffee down on the round timber table and hurriedly brushed a scatter of crimson and gold leaves from a seat. "Here you go."

"Thanks." She settled into her chair and took a sip of her coffee. "This is good." Cradling the mug in her hands, she sent him a smile. "No wonder I don't see you at the Cyprus Cafe."

His heart skipped a beat, shocked that she'd noticed his absence. "I'm usually pretty busy through the week with work, then Saturdays are busy with SES duties and the odd game of social footy. And I don't think the café is open on Sundays, is it?" Now that he thought about it, his life was busier than he'd previously thought.

She shook her head. "I don't think it is."

"And besides, I'm more of a Colombian coffee bean guy. It's sweeter than the Greek brew." He ducked his head, worrying that he sounded like a coffee snob.

"Is that what we're having now? It's lovely. Tastes a bit like chocolate or caramel." She fiddled with the mug handle and shrugged. "As you can tell, I don't know a lot about coffee."

"I'm happy to teach you, if you like. We can try out different flavours while we're building the float." Did he sound too eager? Maybe she wasn't the sophisticated Sydneysider he'd imagined. Perhaps she wasn't out of his league, after all?

"Sure. That sounds like fun."

Her smile was contagious, and he felt his lips curve in response. "Ah, speaking of the float. I thought we could divide up what we need to do. Some of the crew have said they'll help, but everyone's busy, so to be honest, I expect it to be just us."

"That's okay. I think we should be fine on our own." She reached into her satchel and pulled out a sketchbook and pencil. "We have a couple of months, although I don't think we'll need that long, and my time is fairly flexible."

Part of him wanted the project to take that long as an excuse to spend time with her. "I'll give you a key to the shed so that you can come and go as you please if you need to. You won't disturb me. I can make the abseiling rig. Are you able to create a Santa mannequin?"

She tapped her pencil against her lips, a habit she seemed to do while thinking. "Sure, life size?"

"Maybe a bit smaller so the frame doesn't have to be as tall. We can dress him in a pair of SES overalls with the Santa hat and the abseiling harness."

She pulled the sketchbook to her, and within minutes, had sketched out what he'd described. "Something like this?"

The image burst from the page in a simple pencil sketch, exactly as he'd envisioned it.

"Yeah, perfect. And then around the side we could have the native animal cutouts. If you help me draw them, I can cut them out of plywood. Once they're painted, I can fix them to a frame running along the inside of the truck."

She sketched in more of the ideas and swivelled her notebook around to show him a row of kangaroos, koalas and even a goanna that ran along the side of the truck.

"I love it." He sat back and considered. "You're right. I don't think this is going to take as long as we thought, so we can take our time. Would Sunday's work for you? That way it won't interfere with our work or the SES meetings."

"That would be great. Can we start in a couple of weeks? I'm on deadline with the commission I'm currently doing but should have it to the publisher in the next week or so. After that, whatever works for you. I don't have another deadline until later in the year."

"Sure. That works for me." He dared himself to ask what was uppermost in his mind. "No significant other who'll be concerned if you spend time with me on this?"

She shook her head with a wry smile. "No. What about you?"

His heart beat a little faster. "Nope." Spending time together would hopefully deepen their friendship, and after that, maybe there was a chance for it to blossom into something more.

"Good." Their eyes met and held before she settled back in her chair, sipping her coffee with a smile playing on her lips.

For a few minutes, they sat in a comfortable silence, the autumn sun warm on their backs. A magpie fluttered down from the nearby a tree and strutted across the pavers toward them, warbling.

Scott grinned, shaking his head at the bird. "We don't have food. There's no point calling your mates."

Too late. In moments, half a dozen magpies surrounded them, advancing on them with a gleam in their eye.

Kimberley laughed and picked up her phone to film the encounter. "I assume you eat out here a lot?"

He leaned back in his chair and chuckled. "Often enough that they know I usually drop crumbs."

"I can see why you sit out here. It's a gorgeous space, especially with the vines growing over the top." She craned her neck to look up at the timber rafters. "That must give you fantastic shade in summer when the vines aren't bare. Did you build it?"

His shoulders straightened as a warm sensation spread through his chest. "Yeah, with my brother's help."

"You sound close?" With a final warble, the magpies flew away to try their luck elsewhere.

"We are, as much as brothers can be. We're not in each other's pockets, but we see each other fairly regularly." He stared down into the dregs of his coffee, then looked back at her. "It's only the two of us left now that Mum and Dad have both passed on. What about you?"

The light in her eyes dimmed, her smile collapsing. "No siblings. No parents left either. I've got a cousin who I'm quite close to, but that's it now." She shrugged, the movement so small that he wouldn't have seen it if he hadn't been watching her closely. "I'm lucky I have a lot of friends, though. I've made new friends here in Bindarra Creek, and…" She tapped her phone screen. "There are still friends in Sydney who I keep in touch with online."

The smile returned to her eyes. She finished her coffee and placed the mug down on the table. "As much as I'd love to sit here all day, I probably should get back and get organised. I have a full day of work tomorrow." She stood and stowed her sketchbook and pencil back in her satchel. "But thank you for the wonderful coffee. I think we're going to have the best parade float in the town's history."

He rose to his feet, disappointment settling in his gut like a stone as he watched her gather her things. "Do you want to get in touch when you're free to start on it? I can get to work on the A-frame in the meantime. And I'll buy some plywood for the animal cut-outs."

"Good thinking. I'll start gathering things for the mannequin. I'll need a break from my desk at some stage."

He walked beside her down the gravel path, their footsteps falling into a synchronised rhythm. Above them, a cloud drifted across the sun, casting a sudden chill across the land.

Standing in the driveway, he watched her taillights grow smaller until they were swallowed by the bend in the road, leaving only dust motes dancing in the space where she had been. He turned back toward the pergola to gather their empty mugs. She'd only been at his house for a couple of hours, but the silence felt heavier than it ever had before.

Chapter Five

Kimberley breathed a sigh of relief as she sent scans of her finished illustrations off to her publisher. She'd completed the drawings two days ago and taken them to her regular professional scanning service in Tamworth yesterday. While there, she'd treated herself to a coffee and cake at her favourite café, around the corner from the scanning shop. For the first time, she'd taken notice of what type of coffee beans they used and made a mental note to tell Scott.

That wasn't the first time she'd thought of him over the last couple of weeks. He'd popped into her mind often, like when she sat alone in her lounge, scrolling aimlessly through social media at night. And each time she'd added her Scrappy character to another illustration, she remembered him saying he'd look for it in her previous book.

Now that the commission was complete, she could turn her mind to the parade float. It wasn't simply the anticipation of a new creative project that made her heart race at the thought. She felt the promise of something developing between her and Scott. Whether that was a friendship, a creative partnership or a romantic relationship, she wasn't sure, but something was budding.

She shut down her computer, grabbed her keys and stepped out the front door. Casting an anxious look at the steel grey sky, she pulled her coat tighter around her body and hurried to the car. Within minutes, she nosed the vehicle into a parking space near the town's charity op shop. The time had come to get started on the mannequin and what better place to look for materials?

Kimberley made a beeline for the fabric scrap bins, her eyes scanning them for potential treasures. Plunging her hands into the second bin, her fingers brushed against something soft. She tugged gently, working it free from the tangle of materials. A large piece of white fur emerged. Perfect for crafting Santa's bread.

She wandered toward the back of the store, where shelves displayed items kept aside for craft projects. A basket of old stockings caught her attention, and she rummaged through them, searching for pairs sturdy enough to form the mannequin's limbs. Taking a step back, she tilted her head to search the higher shelves, waiting for inspiration to strike.

Her gaze slid past the dummy head before snapping back to it. Perfect! Setting down her gathered items, she stretched up to free it from the top shelf. Probably a hairdresser's mannequin with brittle and teased hair but perfect for Santa's head.

She grinned to herself, and snapped a photo, the mannequin's head nestling against hers like a couple of friends on a girl's night out. For a long moment, her finger hovered over the icon of her messenger app. It was only natural to update her project partner, wasn't it? Mouth dry, she fired off the photo before she over thought it any further.

I found Santa's head.

The bubbles appeared as he typed a response.

Ha! It sounds like you're on some kind of gruesome scavenger hunt.

She reacted with a laugh emoji.

"Uh, excuse me, dear." One of the op shop volunteers attempted to squeeze past her, her arms loaded with donations to go on the shelf.

"Oh, sorry." Kimberley tucked her phone back in her pocket and gathered up her treasures — beard and stockings clutched in one hand, with Santa's mannequin head tucked securely under her arm. She stifled a chuckle, imagining how eccentric she must look, before making her way to the front counter.

"This looks like you're working on something big?" The elderly lady serving smiled at Kimberley, jotting prices on a scrap of paper before placing the items in a bag.

"It's for the Christmas in July parade. I'm helping to decorate the SES float. This will all hopefully form our Santa."

The lady wheezed out a cackle. "We've had a lot of business in here with people looking for clothing and decorations, but you're the first one who's walked out with a head." She handed Kimberley the bag and read out the total.

"I'm sure it's not a common purchase!" Kimberley laughed, handed over cash and took her change. She dumped the bag on the front seat of her car and was about to slide behind the driver's steering wheel when her phone beeped with a message.

Her heart beat a tattoo against her ribs. She opened the messenger app to see a photo from Scott with a half-completed abseiling frame.

Making progress at this end, too.

That looks great. I'm going home to make the rest of Santa's body parts.

She finished with a laugh emoji and drove home.

With the ice broken between them, she found herself eagerly sending update photos throughout the day as Santa took shape. Each message felt more natural than the last as she fashioned limbs from stockings stuffed with newspaper and fabric, meticulously glueing on the white beard and smoothing out the hair to transform the mannequin. By the time she'd added a Santa hat from her own collection and sent Scott another photo of the finished but still naked Santa, their conversation had lasted most of the day.

> I think we'd better get him dressed as soon as possible, or he'll be arrested for indecent exposure.

> Do you have a spare pair of SES overalls for him? Or should I raid the supply cupboard?

> I have some. Would Sunday work for you to come out here and start on the float?

Her cheeks flushed at the thought of seeing Scott again.

> Yes, I'm free. What time?

A long moment passed while she waited anxiously for an answer. Finally, it popped up.

> The weather looks clear for Sunday. Did you want to go bird watching before we start work?

Her grin threatened to split her face.

> I'd like that.

> Do you want to meet out at my place at seven? It's out in the Akuna National Park so it'll probably take us about 30 minutes. Bring your camera.

Fantastic. I'll look forward to it.

How would she fill her time until then? While she had a project she was playing around with, it didn't have a deadline, so she found it difficult to fully immerse herself in it. It would be a long week trying not to get distracted, waiting for Sunday to come.

Scott sat at his kitchen table, watching out the window for Kimberley's car. Ever since he'd made the arrangements with her, the days had dragged.

He took another sip of coffee and checked his watch. The bright spots in the days had been their frequent online conversations. When Kimberley had sent through her progress photos of the Santa mannequin, it had seemed natural to respond with photos of what he was working on.

Gradually, throughout the week, their conversations had turned from the project to more general discussions — the books they were reading, favourite artists, and those small, everyday moments of beauty they both couldn't help but notice. A photo of an autumn leaf she snapped in Lette Park, a shot he'd sent back of the mist hanging on the top of the hills.

He'd never been one much for communicating online, preferring to see people face to face, but his conversations with Kimberley had made him change his mind. For the last few days, he'd checked the phone constantly, eager to keep their connection alive.

Tyres crunched on the gravel, and he shot to his feet. He drained his mug of coffee in one gulp and raced out the back door.

She drew to a halt as she saw him and buzzed down her window. "Hi, where would you like me to park?"

"Normally, the car will be okay here. But round the back of the shed is probably best today since we'll be out for a while. There's a cleared spot there. I'll walk you around."

She crawled alongside him as he walked around to the rear of the shed, indicating with the sweep of his hand where she should park. He forced himself not to hover as she gathered up her goods and stepped out of the car.

"Hi." She smiled and hitched her backpack onto one shoulder. "Looks like it's going to be a nice day. It's still a little bit crisp now." Her voice was quiet in the still morning air.

His hands suddenly felt awkward at his sides, and when their eyes met, a warm flush crept up his neck. "Hopefully, it will warm up soon. Do you want to throw your gear in the ute and grab a coffee to go before we head off?"

She rubbed her hands together. "That would be fantastic. I could do with something warm right now."

He unlocked the ute for her as they walked past it, and she placed her camera bag inside. "Come inside where it's warm while I make the coffee."

Eager to get on the road, it didn't take him long to make up a to-go cup of coffee for them both. He poured the coffee into insulated travel mugs, passing hers to her. "Still Colombian this time, but I've ordered several varieties of beans that should arrive soon."

She took a grateful sip. "Thank you, that's lovely. Forget the float. I might need to be a frequent visitor simply for your coffee." Grinning, she took another sip.

"I'm happy to make you a coffee anytime." The thought brought a smile to his face. Coffee for one was great, but coffee for two would be even nicer sometimes.

Scott picked up his keys from the table. "If you're ready to go, let's get this show on the road."

The drive out to the bird hide seemed to take forever. He was conscious of Kimberley sitting so close to him in the ute, the warmth of her presence making him acutely aware of every movement he made. Her fingers tapped lightly against her thigh to the rhythm of the music he'd turned on low to fill the silence that felt both comfortable and charged with an unspoken anticipation.

He pulled up at the small, cleared parking area, thankful that they had the place to themselves. They stepped out of the ute, the slam of their doors piercing the peaceful quiet, and walked side by side along a wooden boardwalk built above the wetland.

"We're disturbing the frogs." Kimberley whispered the words as she tried to place her feet down lightly. Frogs croaked loudly ahead of them but as they drew nearer, fell silent, trying to stay undetected.

Scott gave a quiet chuckle. "I'm sure they're used to it." He tapped her lightly on the arm to get her attention and then pointed to his right. "See the purple swamphen over there? They look like they're straight out of Jurassic Park."

She raised her camera, focused and fired off several shots of the bird walking across the grasses.

"This is one of my favourite spots." He leaned on the wooden rail, looking out over the wetland, watching the reeds sway gently in the breeze.

"I can see why." She matched his pose, their shoulders brushing. "It's stunning and so peaceful."

His heart swelled that she felt the same way he did. "Wait until we get to the hide. It's not much further."

In a few minutes they reached the weathered timber structure, its sloped corrugated iron roof giving shelter from the elements. He opened the rough-hewn wooden door for her to step inside, holding his breath as she passed close by him.

It was warmer in here, more sheltered from the breeze. She sank down on the bench and peered out through the narrow window.

"This is amazing. How did I not know this was here?"

He felt good that he could show her somewhere new. "It's a fairly well-kept secret. It's part of the Akuna National Park, and the rangers maintain it, but it's kept quiet so that it doesn't attract the wrong type of person."

Sinking down on the bench beside her, he pulled binoculars from his bag. Kimberley busied herself setting up her camera, attaching a long lens to the body.

They kept their voices low and quiet, and for the next hour or so, they didn't speak much other than occasional remarks about the bird life that appeared. Herons and ibises stalked their way through the water on spindly legs, their heads darting into the water in search of food. Several types of ducks swam past, taking off in a flurry of flaps and quacks. Kimberley took shot after shot, seemingly as enthralled as he was.

Normally, Scott could sit here for hours and bird watch without getting distracted, but with Kimberley sitting so close to him, his nerve endings jumped every time she moved. It was hard to find birds when his gaze kept drifting to Kimberley's soft smile, the way her hands cradled the camera, her habit of tucking her hair behind her ears.

He forced his gaze back out to the expanse of water in front of them.

"Look, there's a royal spoonbill." Scott tilted his head towards hers as he pointed toward the far side of the wetland.

The movement brought their shoulders close, and he could feel the warmth emanating from her. She turned her head to respond and suddenly her lips were only an inch away from his, her eyes impossibly blue this close. For a moment, time seemed to freeze. Neither of them backed away. All it would take to kiss her was for him to tilt his head a little to the side...

Another couple blundered into the bird hide, their noise and chatter scaring the birds into flight. Kimberley sent him a pained look.

He didn't know whether to be grateful for the intrusion or not. A kiss could easily have changed so much between them before they were ready to make any transition beyond a working relationship. Needing space, he stood and stuffed his hands into his pockets. "Ready to leave?"

She cast a glance at the intruders and grimaced. "Yeah, we should go back and start working on the float, anyway."

What had almost happened? Had she felt it too? Quietly, they packed up their gear and left the hide to the noisy couple, walking side by side up the path in silence. The air between them felt charged, filled with unspoken questions.

As they reached the ute, Kimberley tucked her bag inside and then turned to him, breaking the tension with a genuine smile that reached her eyes. "That was fantastic. Thank you so much for sharing it with me. I think I got some successful shots, and I can't wait to sketch them."

"You're very welcome." A warm satisfaction spread through him at seeing her enthusiasm for something that meant so much to him.

The atmosphere in the cab carried a charge she couldn't quite identify as they drove back to Scott's house. That moment between them when she'd thought he was going to kiss her had felt so right until the other couple arrived, and now that they were alone again, Kimberley was conscious of his every move. His hands on the steering wheel, the way the sunlight came through the window and highlighted the strands of red in his beard, the curl of his hair at the collar of his shirt.

She'd been in close proximity to many men during her SES training while they adjusted her harness or corrected her hold on the chainsaw. She'd never felt this spark of attraction to any of them.

"Did you notice that pair of crimson rosellas on the way back to the car?" Her voice came out higher than usual. She cleared her throat. "And I think I saw a wedgetail eagle circling overhead. I've never ..." She stumbled over her words as Scott shifted in his seat, his forearm briefly brushing against hers. Her skin tingled at the contact. She tapped her fingers against her knee, counted the trees they passed, anything to keep from staring at the way his profile caught the light. "I've never seen so many varieties in one location before."

She felt a mixture of relief and disappointment when they finally pulled to a halt in Scott's yard. Part of her wished the drive had lasted longer, while another part — the rational, self-preserving part — celebrated the chance to put some distance between them before she did something impulsive she might regret. She fumbled at her feet for her camera bag, dropping it once before managing to grasp the strap, and pushed open the door to break their little bubble.

"Another coffee before we start work?" Scott met her at the back of the ute, brow raised in question.

She wouldn't sleep for a week after this much caffeine, but she seized on the offer to put things back on a normal level. "Thanks."

She followed him into the house and, after freshening up in the bathroom, walked back to the kitchen while Scott prepared the coffee. Taking her camera from the bag, she flicked through the photos she'd taken.

"Oh!" She laughed, delighted with the image on the screen. "Remember that heron we saw catch the fish? I snapped a great shot with the fish caught in his beak."

"Awesome." Scott put down the milk, strolled over to stand beside her and inclined his head. "May I look?"

She angled the camera screen so he could see, but the small display drew him closer than anticipated. Their shoulders touched as he leaned in, his arm settling across hers. The contact sent subtle currents of electricity dancing across her skin. She held her breath, suddenly aware she could have simply handed him the camera instead of creating this moment of intimacy.

"That's an incredible shot. You should enter that one into a competition and see if the gift shop will sell prints of it."

"What a good idea. Thanks. I'll have a chat to the owner." Her voice felt strangled, every word an effort.

He stepped away to grab the coffees. She drew in a deep breath as he handed her the mug, her fingers brushing against his. Looking up, she found his gaze locked with hers in a moment that stretched between them, charged with unspoken possibility. Something kindled in his eyes — a flicker of desire that mirrored her own feelings.

Flustered, she clutched the coffee and retreated a step. He remained motionless for a heartbeat, then blinked as if breaking from a spell, turning back to the counter for his own mug. "I bought the plywood, so I thought we could sketch out the animals today. Then I can cut them out ready for you to paint. You're a much better artist than me, so I'll take my lead from you."

"Yes, but you're used to working at a bigger scale, so I'll need your guidance."

He grinned and kept his gaze on hers. "Sounds like a dream team."

Her heart pounded at his words and the look in his eyes. The phrase hung in the air between them, both innocent and laden with possibility.

Chapter Six

Kimberley glanced at the calendar on her office wall, marking off another day. Nearly a month since she and Scott had begun work on the float. Her desk held a folder of their design sketches, annotated with measurements and colour choices made during those Sundays in his workshop. Six animals complete, another two in progress.

Their collaboration had settled into a comfortable rhythm but stayed firmly within the bounds of friendship. They'd perfected the art of almost-touching — passing tools, reviewing designs, sharing coffee and sandwiches — always stopping short of crossing that invisible line. The float had begun to take shape beautifully while their relationship remained deliberately undefined, despite the undercurrent that still sparked whenever their eyes met.

Opening her email program, she waited for her new emails to load, scanning the subject lines as they appeared.

The Burramys Children's Illustration Prize. Her heart stuttered.

She drew in a deep breath, mentally crossing her fingers, as if that would influence the words in the email. Hands shaking, she opened the message, skimmed the contents, and squealed. She sank into the chair and forced herself to read the email more carefully.

Congratulations. You have been shortlisted for The Burramys Children's Illustration Prize. The ceremony will be held on Tuesday, 15th of July. Please RSVP by 30th of June.

She bounced in her seat, excitement coursing through her as the news sank in. Her first instinct was to message Scott, but she hesitated. Despite the weeks they'd spent working on the float together, she wasn't sure if they'd crossed into sharing-important-news territory yet. Instead, she clicked on her contacts and called her best friend.

"You'll never guess what?"

"You're running off to join the circus?" Jodie laughed.

"No, I'm not nearly flexible enough for that," Kimberley giggled. "I've been shortlisted for the awards."

Jodie's squeal made Kimberley move the phone away from her ear and made her grin spread even wider. It was exciting enough to be nominated, but to have someone else share in those feelings amplified how she felt.

"I feel like celebrating. Are you free for dinner? You and Sean?"

"I'll have to check with him, but I'm definitely free," Jodie said. "At the Riverside?"

"Sounds perfect. We haven't been out for ages. I never feel like it this time of year, between the short days and cold winter nights. I'd prefer to be tucked up at home with the fire going. But tonight is for a celebration."

They settled on a meeting time and hung up. Kimberley sighed. Any attempt at work would be futile today with her mind miles away from the next project. She gifted herself with the day off, filling the hours with mundane tasks; grocery shopping, paying bills, cleaning the house. But no matter what she was doing, her thoughts kept drifting back to the email. The hours crawled by until finally the clock showed it was a reasonable time to leave.

The warm glow of the Riverside Pub welcomed her as she stepped inside, the familiar mingling of conversation and clinking glasses washing over her. She'd barely settled at the entrance when the door swung open again, framing Jodie and Sean as they entered together. Kimberley's heart gave a pang at how right they looked together. They'd only met eighteen months ago when Jodie was housesitting in the area, but they looked like they'd been a couple for decades.

Jodie stepped forward and engulfed her in a hug, while Sean's congratulatory pat landed between her shoulder blades. "Congratulations. We're both so proud of you."

"Thanks." Kimberley smiled at them both. She couldn't imagine her life without their friendship.

They settled at a corner table, debating appetizers with playful jabs about Jodie's aversion to mushrooms and Sean's inexplicable love of anchovies. The friendly argument faded to background noise when Kimberley spotted Scott emerging from Dan's office. Even through the Friday evening crowd with bodies pressed shoulder to shoulder at the bar and waitstaff weaving between tables, his gaze found hers immediately. A soft, hesitant smile crossed his face, warming his features. Without thinking, she raised her hand in invitation, beckoning to him to come over.

Her stomach fluttered with nerves as he approached. These were her closest friends, and Scott was ... well, she wasn't quite sure who Scott would be in her life, but suddenly the idea of these separate worlds colliding felt unexpectedly significant. It felt like a public acknowledgement of her growing feelings; a declaration of a future she hoped would come to pass.

And then he was standing next to her, smiling down, his eyes crinkling at the edges. "Hi."

"Scott, do you know Sean and Jodie?" She swallowed and looked across to meet Jodie's curious gaze.

Scott leaned across the table to shake hands with Sean and gave Jodie a smile. "Hi, I think I've seen you both around town."

Jodie glanced between her and Scott. "Nice to meet you, Scott. How do you two know each other?"

"We're in the SES together. I'm working with Scott on the parade float." Kimberley tripped over her words, not willing to put a concrete name to their relationship.

Jodie's lips quirked. "Ah, I may have heard your name mentioned once or twice over the last few weeks as Kimberley's friend. Actually, we're celebrating her good news. You should join us."

Scott turned to look at Kimberley, his gaze searching her face. "Oh? What's that?"

Kimberley looked down, cheeks on fire, suddenly self-conscious. She chewed on her lower lip. "You know that award I said I was long listed for? I got an email today to say I was shortlisted."

His face lit up with a wide smile. "That's absolutely fantastic. I'm not surprised. Congratulations."

"Thanks." She patted the back of the empty chair, heart racing. "Would you like to join us for dinner? We haven't ordered yet."

He hesitated, then nodded. "That would be wonderful. Saves me going home to cook something. Thanks."

As he settled into the empty chair beside her, she slid her menu across so he could see what was on offer. Sitting at the table next to Scott felt strangely intimate. She hadn't dated anyone since moving to Bindarra Creek. In fact, she hadn't dated anyone for years. Not that this was a date, but it felt closer than anything she'd had for quite a while.

She traced the edge of her menu absently as they placed their orders, the waiter's pen scratching against his notepad. As the waiter disappeared toward the kitchen, she relaxed back into her chair, content to sit back and listen to the discussion that flowed around her as Jodie drew Scott into conversation. He chatted easily with her friends, his smile natural and relaxed. It pleased her that he'd fitted in so easily at their table.

After the waiter delivered their meals to the table, Scott raised his glass in the air. "A toast to Kimberley for her amazing news. Congratulations!"

Her cheeks flushed as her friends raised their glasses, clinking them together. "Thank you all so much." She'd forever be grateful for their support.

As they started on their meals, she turned to Scott. "I saw you come out of Dan's office earlier?"

He beamed. "Yes. I'd been in to talk to him about that commission — the Old Man Jake sculpture. I've got the go-ahead. Just fine-tuning a few details before I get started on it."

She placed her hand on his arm and squeezed. "Why didn't you say so earlier? That's wonderful news. Double celebration!" This time, she raised her glass in a toast to him. "I can't wait to see the finished product."

It seemed like no time at all passed as they finished their meals, their conversation flowing easily. The last bite of apple crumble melted on her tongue as Scott pushed his empty plate away, patting his stomach. "I hate to eat and run, but I've got an early start tomorrow. Thank you so much for inviting me to join you." He stood, fishing in his back pocket for his wallet.

Sean waved him off. "This one's on us. After all, you and Kimberley both had something to celebrate."

"I'll return the favour at some time then. Thanks." Scott smiled at Kimberley as he shrugged on his coat. "Congratulations again. I'll see you on Sunday." He laid a hand lightly on her shoulder as he passed, the warmth lingering after he'd made his way to the door.

"Time for us to head off too." Jodie started gathering her things as Sean headed for the cash register to pay. After a quick glance that he was out of earshot, she grinned at Kimberley. "That's Scott, then, hmm? Only a friend? I think we need a proper catch-up soon."

Kimberley blushed. "After yoga next week?"

"Be ready to spill the beans." Jodie winked, then turned to meet her partner.

Kimberley fell into step behind them as they left, Sean's hand steady on Jodie's lower back as they navigated between tables. All things considered, it had gone well. Better than well, really. Scott had fit in like he'd always been part of their little group.

Her phone buzzed with a message from Scott.

> *Thanks for tonight. Your friends are lovely.*

She smiled as she drove home, wondering if she dared hope for more than friendship.

Scott pushed open the workshop door on Sunday morning right as Kimberley pulled into the driveway.

"Perfect timing." He waited until she climbed out of her car, then handed her a mug of coffee. "Try this. I got some new beans through the week."

She accepted the mug gratefully, wrapping her cold hands around it. "What am I tasting today?"

"It's an Ethiopian blend." He watched as she took a tentative sip. "It's supposed to have floral notes with a hint of chocolate."

Her nose wrinkled. "Hmm, it's a bit different from what we had before, but I think it could grow on me."

"I bought a few other varieties as well. By the time the parade rolls around, you'll be an aficionado." He grinned at her sceptical expression. "Speaking of which, my turn to choose the music."

"I don't think so." She followed him into the workshop, cradling her coffee. "You played nothing but country last time. My ears need a break from all that twanging."

"Twanging? That was classic Australian country!" He mock-glared at her. "And if I recall correctly, you were singing along to Slim Dusty by lunchtime."

"I think you're mistaken." She grinned, reaching for her phone. "But it's still my turn."

He rolled his eyes with an exaggerated sigh. "Fine. But if it's show tunes again, I'll queue up my death-metal playlist next week."

She laughed and connected her phone to the Bluetooth speaker. The opening notes of Billy Joel's *Piano Man* filled the workshop. She'd obviously taken his threat about the show tunes seriously.

They set to work where they'd left off — Kimberley painting one of the characters he'd cut out while he was busy building a frame to fit to the inside of the truck tray. He stopped work for a minute to watch her, the brush moving with confident strokes, bringing the animal figure to life with vibrant colours.

"I enjoyed Friday night. Thanks for inviting me." He had really enjoyed spending time with her friends, seeing a different side to her. "Your friends are nice."

"They are." Kimberley looked up, paintbrush held in the air. "Jodie and I hit it off when she was looking after Stevie's cottages a couple of years ago. And thankfully, she decided to stay in the area."

"Congratulations again on your shortlisting." He'd already said it a dozen times, but he liked the way it made her smile and brought a blush to her cheeks. "When's the award ceremony?"

"It's about a month away." Even from a distance, he could see the way her eyes sparkled.

"I bet you're excited."

"I am, not only for the ceremony, but it will be nice to be back in Sydney for a change. I might catch up with some friends while I'm there." Her eyebrows lifted as she had a sudden thought. "Oh, I'll check what's on at the theatre. The local amateur theatrical society does some good shows, but it's not quite the same as seeing a national theatre company."

Her face glowed with each thing that she described, the paintbrush suspended in mid-air as she spoke of art galleries and harbourside restaurants. As her face grew brighter, Scott's heart sank deeper. The screwdriver in his hand felt heavier, each movement an effort.

It looked like Bindarra Creek could never compete with the lure of Sydney. It hadn't been enough for his ex-wife, and it seemed like Kimberley would relocate there in a second, given the chance.

And who knew what opportunities this shortlisting would open for her? Particularly if she won. She might move back to Sydney quicker than he thought.

He couldn't deny his feelings for Kimberley grew each day they spent together working on the float. The more he got to know her, the stronger his feelings grew. It wasn't simply a physical attraction — although he was definitely attracted to her — but he hadn't connected with anyone like this for so long. Someone who could understand his vision and accept the time he spent on his creative pursuits, when he could stick to functional, boring welding. But any thoughts he'd had that a relationship might be in their future were being dashed the more she spoke about the delights of the big city.

Sitting back on his haunches, he watched her apply a sandy brown paint to the wombat, a smudge of paint transferring to her cheek. The urge to wipe it away, to touch her at all, hit him hard.

He vowed to himself to put his feelings back where they belonged — in a box — and instead enjoy their friendship for as long as it lasted.

Chapter Seven

L ater that week, Kimberley caught herself humming a country music song as she walked to her yoga class. She cut herself off mid-chorus, shaking her head. Scott's country music obsession was apparently contagious. As she walked into the CWA hall, she forced thoughts of him out of her mind. He'd been occupying far too much space there lately for her peace of mind.

She strolled over to where Jodie sat on her mat, twisting her upper body to warm up. Kimberley unrolled her yoga mat, making a smacking sound as it unfolded and slapped on the wooden floor. Her friend straightened and smiled up at her.

"Hey, you."

"Hi." She sank down onto her mat and pushed her legs out in front of her, bending her upper body into a stretch.

Jodie leaned across. "After class, you need to give me the scoop on you and Scott." Her loud whisper carried to the woman beside them.

Still prone, Kimberley twisted her head to face her friend. She'd been hoping Jodie would have forgotten her promise to grill her. "What do you mean? What scoop?" She struggled to keep her voice casual.

"You looked pretty cosy the other night. Is there something else going on that I should know about?"

Tessa clapped her hands and drew their attention to begin the class. *Saved by the bell!*

"Want to walk along the river after?" Kimberley whispered across the gap, struggling to her feet to stand at the end of her mat for the warmup.

"Good plan. We need to take advantage of the nice morning while we can."

Kimberley had missed a few yoga sessions lately, and her body let her know it throughout the class. Her hamstrings protested as she folded forward, and her back creaked when she reached into downward dog. After spending far too long hunched over the desk, it was nice to feel the knots in her neck and shoulders release with each stretch.

"Remember to breathe into those tight spots," Tess called out, walking between their mats. "Let go of whatever you're holding onto."

Kimberley stifled a chuckle. There were far too many tight spots. If she breathed into all of them, she'd hyperventilate.

By the time they moved into the final relaxation pose, her muscles felt loose and languid, though she knew she'd undoubtedly be sore tomorrow.

After final *namastes*, she rolled up her mat and tucked it under her arm. The group arranged to head to the café for brunch but, with a glance at Jodie, Kimberley made their apologies.

"I'll give you a lift up to the river and you can leave your mat in my car, if you like?" Jodie picked up her backpack and reached for the keys in the front pocket.

"Thanks." They farewelled the class and walked outside. Kimberley climbed into Jodie's car, tossing her yoga mat on the backseat. They chatted about the class for the few minutes it took to drive to the river, then fell silent as they headed to the walking trail.

They strolled along the river path, the winter sun casting long shadows through the gum trees. Kimberley pulled her cardigan tighter as they moved into a shaded section, the sudden chill making her shiver. The river flowed quietly beside them, the surface rippling in the breeze.

Jodie looked around to make sure they were alone before grabbing Kimberley's arm. "You and Scott. Am I right that there is something between you two?"

Kimberley kept her eyes on the path ahead, watching a family of ducks waddle toward the water. "I don't know. I think so. I hope so. Maybe." She shook her head. "I'm confused. There've been moments when I thought something might happen, but then nothing. I get the feeling that he's interested in me, but he hasn't made a move at all."

"And what about you? Does he tickle your fancy? Float your boat?"

A warmth spread through her that had nothing to do with emerging back into the sunshine. "Yeah, he does actually. He's a really sweet guy. Gentle and so creative. We've hit it off talking about art, and it's like he gets me."

"Well, why not ask him out? You don't need to wait for him."

Kimberley stopped walking and leaned against the railing overlooking the river. "I don't know if I can do it again. I'll be honest, I wasn't great at being married. I'd disappear into my own head too much, spend too much time on my art rather than doing things together as a couple. It was a relief when we got divorced and I only had myself to please."

Jodie came to stand beside her, their shoulders almost touching.

"I don't know if I'll be any good at being in a relationship. I'm sixty. Am I too old?" She laughed. "It seems a bit silly."

Jodie whirled to face her, wagging her finger in mock outrage. "So, it was all right for Sean and me to get together when we were that age? Did you think we were too old?"

"No, no, of course not, but you two seemed like the perfect match."

"Well, I think you should open yourself to the possibility that maybe Scott is your perfect match." Jodie bumped her shoulder gently. "You're both creative. If anyone is going to understand disappearing into your own head, surely it's another creative person. And you have to admit he's pretty easy on the eye."

Kimberley fought the smile that was playing at her lips. "Theoretically, I guess I could admit that he is quite attractive." The truth was, he stirred feelings in her that she thought were long dormant. Simply watching his hands as he worked made her wonder what they'd feel like on her skin.

"Well, I think you should take a chance." Jodie linked her arm through Kimberley's, and they started walking again. "I don't think you're ever too old for a second chance at love."

A kookaburra laughed in the distance as they rounded the bend, and for a moment, Kimberley let herself imagine what that second chance might look like.

Although Scott's last two weeks had been quite busy, he hadn't been able to stop himself thinking about Kimberley. With every cut and weld on his magpie sculpture for the park, thoughts of her filled his mind. Despite it reminding him of their night out with her friends, he'd also made good progress on the statue of Old Man Jake to stand outside the Riverside Pub. The old bloke had been such a fixture at the pub that it still felt odd to not see him propping up the bar when Scott went in. The statue, with Curly the cockatoo on his shoulder, would be a fitting tribute.

Despite his vow to tuck his feelings away, his heart still stuttered every time she sent a message showing her latest work or sharing a funny story she'd heard in town. In turn, he'd shared progress photos of his magpie sculpture, alongside photos of his nephews reading one of her books. Last week he'd driven up towards Moree to pick up an old wooden bench for his Old Man Jake statue to rest on. He'd spotted a cute blue wren family and sent her a video because he knew she'd love it.

If a day went by without hearing from her, his spirits would sink. Even his brother had commented that he'd been more distracted by his phone than normal.

But finally, they were back working on the float together. Through the week, Kimberley had driven out to Tamworth to collect a huge box of second-hand Christmas decorations from someone selling them online, and now it was Scott's job to transform their float with a festive spirit.

He pulled a long strand of red and green tinsel from the box. "No wonder you had to drive so far to buy these. The town has really gone all out, haven't they? I'm surprised there are any decorations left within a hundred-k radius."

"You're not a fan of the decorations?" There was a teasing lilt to her voice, but her eyes held genuine curiosity.

"Not really." He hesitated with his fingers still wrapped in tinsel, then he blurted out a confession he hadn't told many people. "Christmas still has some bad memories for me. A few years after I got married, I woke up on Christmas morning to find that my wife wasn't in the bedroom and something felt ... off. I walked out to the kitchen and there was a note on the table. A *Dear John* letter. She'd decided to move to the city. She'd had enough of living in Bindarra Creek."

Kimberley stopped painting and put down her brush to stare at him, her mouth parting in shock. "Seriously? That must have really hurt."

He shrugged, trying to mask the old ache. "Yeah, it took me a long time to get over it. I'm glad we didn't have kids like we'd been planning. That would have ruined me." He fell silent for a few minutes, methodically sorting through the box of decorations, separating the tinsel bunches and making piles of baubles on the workbench. "Now you know my secret."

Kimberley stood silent for a moment, sadness flickering across her face. "I'm sorry it didn't work out for you. Christmas should be a time of celebration not loss." She sighed as she moved to stand beside him at the bench. "I was about six months pregnant one Christmas. We'd only been married for a couple of years and were really excited about our baby. Then I miscarried. We lost our baby boy. His name was Toby." She gave a sad smile that didn't reach her eyes. "Rather than letting myself sink into depression, I decided to embrace Christmas — for all the ones Toby couldn't have."

"I'm so sorry." Words seemed inadequate. He covered her hand with his as she leaned closer, their shoulders touching for a heartbeat before she moved away again.

"Thanks. It was a long time ago. But that's why I love Christmas so much. Speaking of which ..." She picked up her phone and opened her music app. "I think we need Christmas carols to work by today."

He groaned but didn't object when *All I want for Christmas* filled the air. She deserved to play carols all day, every day if it made her happy.

She returned to painting while he untangled a stubborn string of outdoor Christmas lights. He could hook them up to a spare car battery and really deck their float out with flashing Christmas spirit.

Finally, Kimberley stretched, wandered over to her backpack and pulled out two packets of crisps. "Break time." She tossed him one and then wandered outside the shed. They sat side by side on an old bench he'd added near the door.

She bumped him lightly with her shoulder. "Do you at least have good memories of Christmas as a kid?"

He hadn't thought about that for years. He cast his mind back and began to laugh. "You know what? I do. There was the one Christmas when my brother and I decided to wait up for Santa. We must've been about eight and ten. We rigged up this ridiculous alarm system with string and empty tins across the front door, determined to catch him in the act. Of course, we fell asleep on the lounge room floor, and Dad tripped over our booby trap at four in the morning when he came in to put the presents out. The crash woke the whole house."

Kimberley laughed, the sound ringing out across the land, making him laugh too. "What did your father do?"

"He pretended that he'd come out to see what the noise was and said we must have frightened Santa away." He chuckled. "Geez, we were innocents. We totally fell for his explanation."

"Or maybe you wanted to keep believing for a little longer. What else do you remember?"

"Oh, Mum would always make way too much pavlova, claiming it was for the neighbours, but we'd end up eating most of it ourselves. We made ourselves so sick, but it was worth it." He smiled at the memories. "Thanks for reminding me of all that. I'd forgotten how much fun Christmas used to be."

As he said goodbye a couple of hours later and watched her drive away, his heart felt lighter than it had in years. She'd managed to obliterate the darkness surrounding his Christmas memories and opened the way for his more cherished ones to shine through. And now he couldn't wait to start creating new ones. Hopefully with her by his side.

Chapter Eight

With less than a week before the parade, Kimberley drove the now familiar road out to Scott's house. The heavy clouds were slate grey in the morning light, dark and threatening. The wind was already picking up as she parked and walked around to the shed. Leaves and other debris whipped past, hitting against the workshop with a *ting*.

She slid the door open and stepped inside, her body soaking up the warmth after the biting chill outside. Large heaters mounted on the walls cast a radiant glow, their orange light flickering against the windows of the truck. The top of Scott's head was partly visible on the far side of the vehicle.

"Good morning." She slid the door shut, cocooning them in the warmth. "That weather's not looking great. I'll finish what I can as quickly as possible and then head home."

Scott raised his head over the cab of the truck. "Morning. Sure, no problem. We're coming to the end of it, anyway. There's not too much to do now."

She walked to the workbench, slung her backpack underneath and gathered up her painting tools. "Great, because I have to drive to Sydney tomorrow for Tuesday's award ceremony."

A weight settled in her stomach at the thought of the project ending. No more excuses to see Scott regularly. Would their online friendship trail off as well once they had no reason to stay connected?

The thought of not having her days brightened by a message from Scott made her chest ache. She treasured the friendship they'd developed — the easy rhythm while working together, their shared laughter, the way their combined creativity sparked ideas bigger than they could have conceived individually. She felt that rare connection of two minds that spoke the same language, even if his taste in music left a lot to be desired.

More than that, she wanted a chance to discover if the friendship they'd built could grow into something deeper, something that wouldn't end after the Christmas in July parade.

Pushing the thought from her mind, she rolled up her sleeves and looked over at the truck to see their progress. The concept had grown as they'd worked. From the original design of a row of animals surrounding the outside, the tray was now mostly filled with animal cut-outs, with the occasional elf scattered throughout. Scott stood on the tray in the remaining space, attaching her mannequin to the abseiling frame he'd built.

Kimberley smiled at the sight of the mannequin, wearing bright orange SES overalls, sturdy work boots and a jaunty Santa hat perched at an angle. "That looks great. I think the kids will love it."

The thought lifted her spirits. If nothing else, they'd created something special that the town would love. Maybe they could donate the cutouts after the parade was done. Surely, the council or the school would enjoy them for future Christmas events?

Scott jumped down from the back of the truck, dusting off his hands. The corner of his mouth twisted in a smirk. "They'll probably love the lollies that we're throwing out even more."

She laughed and knelt by the plywood cutout, ready to pick up where she'd finished last time. Scott strolled over to the workbench and switched on the Bluetooth speaker. "I have a surprise. Today we don't need to argue over control of the music."

"Hmm?"

"I made a playlist last night. It's a mix of both of our tastes. Although adding the show tunes nearly broke me."

Tears sprang to her eyes at the sweet gesture, but she forced a smile. "I'll bet you've added more country than anything else. No death metal, I hope?"

He threw his head back and laughed. "No, no death metal. And I swear I tried to make the mix even."

"I guess we'll see." She smiled as she uncapped the paint tin and poured out enough to finish painting the small swamp wallaby.

He started the playlist. "Oh, you'll love this one."

Kimberley rolled her eyes when the opening guitar twangs of a country song filled the shed. She refused to admit she'd actually started to enjoy it.

They worked companionably, discussing the other festivities the CWA had planned for the month and the influx of tourists it had brought to the town. True to his word, the playlist was varied — Elton John mixing with Cold Chisel, songs from The Greatest Showman giving way to Keith Urban tunes. Despite the occasional glance that lingered a moment too long, they said nothing about where they'd go from here.

Without warning, the lights flickered once, twice and plunged them into dimness. The sudden silence as the music cut out was jarring, the void instantly filled by the rush of wind outside, rattling the shed with growing intensity.

Kimberley glanced at her watch, barely visible in the weak light coming in through the high windows. "Oh no. I lost track of time. It's later than I'd planned to stay. I guess that's my cue to leave."

"It doesn't sound good out there. Hopefully, the power comes back on soon." He glanced up at the heaters, ticking as they cooled down. "It's going to get freezing cold in here soon. Come inside the house and I'll check the warnings before you head home."

She cleaned her brushes as well as she could in the fading light, wincing as the cold water hit her skin. The chill from the concrete floor travelled up through her boots and, as she put away the paints, she stamped her feet to warm them. Meanwhile, Scott moved methodically through the shed, tidying and making sure everything was switched off for when the power eventually returned.

"Ready?"

At her nod, Scott slid open the door. The wind rushed into the opening with an angry howl, blowing hard against the shed. A small tree branch skittered along the path in front of her, weaving erratically in the gusts. Scott struggled to force the door closed against the pressure, his muscles straining, before he finally slid it shut. He took her arm, his grip firm but gentle, supporting her as they fought the wind together to reach the house. The dark clouds had turned menacing overhead, heavy spots of rain already peppering the ground in warning of the downpour to come.

Stepping into the kitchen brought a respite from the cutting chill of the wind. The house had some residual warmth from the overnight fire, and her fingers tingled as they soaked in the heat.

"Can I quickly use your bathroom?"

"Of course. You know where it is. I'll stoke up the stove."

Kimberley visited the bathroom and quickly joined Scott in the warm kitchen. The storm picked up in ferocity, rain pounding against the roof. Leaning against the counter, Scott studied his phone with a furrowed brow. Drawn to the comforting warmth, she crossed to stand closer to the wood-fired stove, holding out her hands toward the heat.

He glanced up from his phone and shook his head. "It looks like the storm is about to get even worse. How about you stay here for a little while until it passes?"

"Thank you. I'd prefer not to drive in it if possible."

"I'll put the kettle on the stove. We'll have to stick with instant for now." He looked mournfully at his now-useless coffee machine, picked up the stovetop kettle and carried it to the sink. "I knew I should have bought that French press. Take a seat in the lounge room. I'll light the fire in there once I put the kettle on. By the look of the storm, we're done outside for the day."

Kimberley wandered into his living room and sank down onto the sofa. Gosh, it was comfy. For a second, she imagined herself relaxing here with Scott after their workdays were over, book in hand, in front of the crackling fire. It was a very seductive thought — and not simply because the sofa was so comfy.

A few minutes later, Scott came in and knelt in front of the open fireplace, already built for a new fire. She watched the confident movements of his hands as he struck a match to the pile which caught easily, flames licking up through the kindling. Within minutes, the fire gave off a faint heat that began to chase away the lingering chill from her bones.

"Coffee won't be long. Can I tempt you with a pan-toasted sandwich since it's near enough to lunchtime? I have ham, cheese and tomato, if any of those appeal to you."

"Actually, that all sounds fabulous. Thank you. Can I help?"

"No, you stay here and enjoy the fire. I won't be long."

She tried to relax, aware of him moving around in the room next door — cupboard doors banging, the shriek of the kettle as it came to the boil, pans clattering. Closing her eyes, she drifted off into another daydream, picturing this as their normal routine.

At the clunk of a tray hitting the coffee table, her eyes flew open. She sat up straight and surreptitiously wiped her mouth in case she'd drifted off and drooled.

"Here you go. The finest in quality dining." He handed across a plate topped with a delicious looking toastie.

Her senses filled with the comforting smell of thick buttery bread and caramelised cheese edges mixed with the sharp aroma of coffee. Her mouth watered. "Smells great. Thanks."

"You're welcome." He sat on the sofa beside her, his knees brushing hers. The casual contact sent a warmth through her that had nothing to do with the growing fire.

"Do we have much left to do on the float? I'm on the last cutout so I'll have to finish that when I get back from Sydney." She bit into her sandwich, waving a hand in front of her mouth as the hot tomato hit her tongue.

"Only tinkering left for me, I think. Hooking up the Christmas lights and screwing on those cutouts you finished today." He nudged his knee against hers. "We've done a good job."

A soft glow unfurled through her body, both at his touch and his words. "We work well together."

"We do." He stared intently at his sandwich. "I wonder ... maybe we could collaborate on future projects? For work, I mean?"

"I'd like that." Her pulse quickened at the possibility that Scott wanted to continue their connection as well.

They fell silent as they finished their lunch. She stared into her coffee, cradling the mug for warmth, hyperaware of his presence beside her. Outside, the wind howled around the house and rain lashed against the windows, the storm creating a cocoon around them.

She glanced sideways at him, his mug in one hand, the other scrolling through his phone. The dancing flames cast his features in a soft, golden glow.

"Oh, that's not good. I've got a text from Roman. It looks like there's a tree down over the road into town, possibly more than one."

"Are you on call? Do you need to go?"

"He said they're okay for now. The creek's rising fast, so he said to stay put. Enough of the crew is available closer to town to cover."

"How long do they think it will last? When will I be able to go home?"

He shook his head. "It doesn't look like letting up for the rest of the day. I think you're stuck here. Looks like you'll need to stay here for the night."

Her heart stuttered, a wave of heat rushing over her and then receding. "Stay here?"

"It's too dangerous to drive back into town. The emergency app is forecasting flash flooding." He shifted slightly in his seat to face her. "I have a spare room. You'll be safer here."

Physically she might be safer, but emotionally? She trusted Scott, but what about her heart? She was already in danger of wanting more from this relationship than friendship.

Scott stared at the emergency alert, holding his breath, waiting for her response.

"Oh." Her voice was soft. "Thanks. I hate to be a bother."

"No bother."

Kimberley. Staying the night. Under his roof. The thought ricocheted through him, setting off alarms and desire in equal measure.

He drew a steadying breath, willing his expression to remain neutral. The last thing he needed was for her to see how the prospect of her spending the night had knocked him sideways. How many times had he imagined her here, in his space, not as a friend passing through, but staying?

The crackling of the fire and the cosiness as the storm raged outside already had him thinking thoughts that he couldn't admit to.

He had to move. Had to put distance between them. He rose to put more wood on the fire, even though it didn't need it.

She jumped up from the sofa. "Mind if I take a look at your bookcase?"

"Help yourself." Tension replaced the cosiness of their situation. It shouldn't be that way. They were friends, right? Surely they could spend the night under the same roof like adults.

As he busied himself unnecessarily with the fire, she chose a paperback and settled back down on the sofa.

"Do you have enough light to read there?"

"It's fine for now. Thanks."

"I'll get the gas lamps ready, anyway. We'll need them soon unless the power comes back on." Light faded fast from the room, hastened by the storm outside making it feel hours later than it was.

Scott hurried out to his laundry, shivering as he opened the door into the room. He'd closed the doors to keep the warmth from the fires contained in the rooms they were using, rather than heating unnecessary spaces. It was so cold he could see his breath forming as he exhaled. Thank goodness for his wood-burning heating.

He reached into the cupboard and pulled out his box of emergency supplies. Power cuts were all too common living out of town, so he'd learnt early on to keep the box topped up with all he'd need to survive for a few days. Hopefully the cuts wouldn't last that long this time.

Pulling the laundry door shut behind him, he carried the box into the kitchen, set it down on the counter, and then pulled out one of the gas lanterns. Despite Kimberley's statement that she could see fine, he lit one and carried it into the living room, anyway. They'd need one soon.

She glanced up as he placed the lantern on the coffee table, gave him a grateful smile, before returning to her book. He could see from the cover that she'd chosen one of his John Grisham novels. Were legal thrillers her usual preference? He was tempted to ask but kept his curiosity to himself. After all, it annoyed him when he was interrupted mid-reading session.

He picked up his own book from the coffee table and opened it at the bookmark. The words swam before his eyes while Kimberley sat only an arm's length away. Each rustle as she turned pages, each subtle shift of her weight on the cushions beside him, tore his attention back to her. But gradually, mercifully, the escapades of Jack Reacher drew him in.

When she stirred beside him, it jolted him back to reality with an unexpected force. How could he have forgotten she was there? It felt so right to have her sitting next to him, like an old married couple relaxing after a hard day's work.

She stretched. "I don't think the power is going to come on anytime soon. And the storm doesn't seem to be letting up."

He glanced at his watch. "Are you hungry? I could cook." He laughed. "Actually, 'cook' might be a bit of an overstatement. I have a couple of frozen pizzas I can throw in the Aga's oven, if that will do you."

She smiled. "Good to see I'm not the only one who lives on frozen convenience foods."

"I can cook, but —" He shrugged.

She finished his thought. "But it's such a pain when it's cooking for one. I love throwing dinner parties for friends, but when it's only me, it's much easier to toss something in the oven or microwave."

He nodded, relieved that she understood. There was something intimate about finding these small connections. He enjoyed cooking when the mood took him, but his preference and expertise leaned more toward tossing a steak on the barbeque than cooking a gourmet meal.

"Can I help?"

"No, it will only take me a few minutes to unwrap them and throw them in the oven. It shouldn't take long to cook."

Alone in the kitchen, he unwrapped the pizzas, placed them onto a baking tray, and slid them into the oven. He set the kitchen timer hanging on the fridge and walked back into the living room.

Kimberley relaxed on the sofa, her book in her lap, staring into the flames. With a start, she sat upright and clasped a hand to her mouth. "I forgot Tibbles!"

"Sorry?" He perched on the seat beside her. "Who or what is a Tibbles?"

She chuckled. "Tibbles is my cat. He'll be waiting for his dinner."

"Is there someone you can phone? Do you have a neighbour who could call in and feed him?"

Grimacing, she shook her head. "I haven't left a spare key with anyone, and I lock up when I'm not home." She tapped her finger against her bottom lip. "He's an inside cat. He has dry food and water, but he's very demanding, so he'll be expecting wet food."

Scott reached across the space between them and placed a hand on her arm. At some stage through the afternoon, she'd taken off her jacket and her soft skin was warm under his palm. The contact was meant to comfort her, but it bridged the careful distance they'd maintained, and his mouth went dry.

"I'm sure he'll be fine. Cats are very resilient." His voice came out lower than he'd intended.

Her gaze dropped to where his hand rested against her skin. The seconds stretched, but she made no move to pull away. "Yes, but he will give me a mouthful of cheek when I go back home tomorrow. Especially since I have someone popping in to feed him while I'm away over the next few days." She laughed. "I definitely won't be in his good books when I get back from Sydney."

As her laughter faded, the room seemed to grow impossibly still. He knew he should remove his hand, but it felt like he was frozen in place. His thumb moved almost imperceptibly against her forearm.

She drew in an uneven breath that he felt more than heard. Almost in slow motion, she reached out and covered his hand with hers.

His heart hammered against his ribs. Such a simple touch — fingertips against knuckles — but it carried the weight of unspoken questions, of possibilities neither had dared voice.

When she squeezed his hand gently, something shifted in the air between them. Her touch gave him courage. He turned his hand over, palm upward in silent invitation. Their fingers hovered centimetres apart — a precipice neither had dared crossed before. His eyes never left her face as he slowly, cautiously, interlaced his fingers with hers, each point of contact igniting nerve endings he hadn't known existed.

She stared back at him, a soft smile playing around her lips that suddenly seemed the focus of his entire world. The pressure of her fingers tightening around his sent waves of electricity up his arm. She made no move to break the connection, their hands remaining intertwined in this new, fragile reality.

His heart hammered against his ribs. Did she feel the same longing? Would she risk their comfortable friendship for something deeper?

The pulse pounding in his ears drowned all other sounds. "Would you —"

He froze as the persistent beeping from the kitchen timer finally penetrated their little bubble.

A curse formed under his breath, barely audible. The courage that had carried him across the boundary between friendship and something more evaporated with each chirp. Would he find that bravery again, or had the moment been lost?

"That sounds like the pizza." Her voice was slightly breathless.

He stood, fingers lingering against hers for one last precious second, before reluctantly breaking apart. The loss of her warmth was like a stab to the guts as he moved toward the kitchen, each step widening the physical distance between them while his mind stayed fixed on the memory of her hand in his.

Chapter Nine

Kimberley let out her breath when the timer beeped, and Scott walked to the kitchen. The living room seemed suddenly emptier without him. Her hand tingled where his had rested, a phantom warmth that lingered like the flow of the flames.

At sixty, she'd resigned herself to a life without that flutter in her chest. But here it was again, awakened by the touch of Scott's callused hands. When he'd covered her hand with his, a delicious shiver had travelled from her wrist to her shoulder and down her spine.

In that suspended moment before the timer interrupted them, Scott's eyes had held hers with an intensity that made her breath catch. He'd started to say something. An invitation, perhaps? An opportunity to take the next step in their relationship?

Life had taught her that opportunities rarely knocked twice. Next time, if he hesitated, she would have to be brave enough to bridge the gap herself.

She smiled to herself, listening to him moving about in the kitchen. They were well past the giddy romance of youth, but this could be something richer, deeper. Two independent, creative souls, drawn together to enrich their lives.

Scott appeared at the doorway, holding plates and waving a handful of cutlery in the air. "I wasn't sure if you needed these for pizza or not?"

She wrinkled her nose. "No, I'm not the delicate type. Hands do just as well for me."

He laughed and placed the plates on the coffee table, then arranged a couple of heat mats beside them that he'd had tucked under his arm. "I'll grab the pizzas. Back in a sec."

He disappeared and a minute later, true to his word, appeared with the pizzas on baking trays, the aroma of tomato and spices wafting from them.

Kimberley's stomach growled in response. "These look good!"

"They may be frozen pizza, but I do only buy the best." He placed the trays on the coffee table and bowed like a butler.

She laughed and pulled a couple of slices onto her plate. Reaching over, she lifted the other plate and offered it to Scott. Their fingers brushed through the exchange — a fleeting touch that might once have been accidental but now held unmistakable intention. Their eyes met and locked, the air between them growing dense with anticipation. A pleasant warmth spread through her body.

With a shy smile, he broke contact and stooped to pick up his own slices. He sank back onto the sofa beside her. Was he perhaps sitting a little closer than before? Or was she now even more conscious of the heat of his body radiating out beside her?

Food first and then tackle whatever was growing between them.

They ate in a charged silence, loud with unspoken words. Each time they reached for another slice, they nudged closer to each other. By the time they finished the pizzas, there was little space separating the two of them.

Kimberley placed her plate down on the coffee table and wiped her hands and mouth on the paper serviette. "Thank you, that was very delicious!"

He grinned. "That might be exaggerating slightly, but you're welcome."

She let her hand flutter past his knee, then sat back against the cushions, deliberately brushing his leg as she settled. Her hand came to rest upturned on her thigh — hopefully, the invitation was loud and clear.

He placed his own plate on the coffee table with careful deliberation. The sofa dipped slightly as he eased back against her, their shoulders nearly touching. Then, with a casualness that contradicted the significance of the gesture, he reached across and took her hand in his, his fingers sliding between hers as naturally as if they had always sat like this.

For now, this was enough — this connection, this acknowledgement of mutual desire. She was content to sit beside him, feeling the weight of his palm against hers, the tension building between them. His thumb traced lazy circles across her palm, each movement sending nerve endings ricocheting around her body.

Her skin hummed with awareness, a flush rising from somewhere deep within.

She turned her head to find him watching her, his eyes soft with an emotion she hadn't seen directed her way for far too long. Her heart threatened to pound out of her chest.

Drawing in a deep breath, she gathered her courage. "You were about to say something before?" The words hung between them, fragile and vulnerable.

His gaze dropped away, focusing somewhere on her joined hands, and her heart plummeted. Had she misread the situation? Was she being too forward?

She held her breath and waited for him to pull away, to retreat into the safety of their friendship.

Scott dropped his eyes from Kimberley's, unable to think while he gazed into her eyes. He drew in a steadying breath, then met her waiting gaze again.

"You know …" He shrugged, his hands suddenly feeling too large, too rough in her delicate grasp. "Actually, you probably don't know. I've had a crush on you since you joined the SES." He frowned. "Are we too old to use the word 'crush'? Whatever. I've liked you since the day I met you."

He stared into her eyes, hoped he could find the right words. "But I've been scared to say anything. I didn't think you'd feel the same way. I didn't think you ever noticed me — not really."

"I noticed you." The firelight played across her face, highlighting the sparkle in her eyes. "The polite man who did what he said and was always reliable, always willing to help. They're good qualities, in my opinion." She squeezed his hand, her thumb tracing the callus at the base of his palm.

Her hands were so soft compared to his that he wondered what she thought. Did she mind? The thought made him self-conscious, but he couldn't bring himself to pull away.

"But these last couple of months, I've gotten to know you." Her face lit up in a dazzling smile. "And I have to say, whether we use the term or not, I've got a crush on you, too."

His breath caught in his throat as her words sank in, a warmth spreading from his chest to his fingertips. Relief crashed over him, followed by a surge of joy that made his heart stutter in his chest. This was really happening. When he'd resigned himself to a life of quiet solitude, life had thrown him this magnificent curveball. "Would you like to go on a date with me sometime? A real one, not one where I'm putting you to work." The steadiness of his voice surprised him.

Her lips curved in a smile that reached all the way to her eyes, crinkling the corners in a way that made his heart skip. "I thought you'd never ask."

He lifted his free hand, hesitating for only a moment before gently pushing a strand of hair away from her face, his fingertips grazing the softness of her cheek. "Would it be too forward to kiss you before we have our first date? I don't want you to think I'm easy."

A peal of laughter rang out, genuine and unrestrained. "I promise I won't hold it against you." Her eyes danced with anticipation. "You have my permission."

He leaned forward slowly, holding her gaze, savouring each second. His heart thumped in his chest like this was his first kiss. And in some ways, it was. The first kiss of this new chapter, this unexpected gift of a second chance at romance.

She leaned forward as well, her eyes fluttering closed, a gesture of trust that touched him deeply. He brushed his lips against hers, tentatively at first, then with growing certainty as she responded. The kiss deepened, and he sank into the sensation, marvelling at how right it felt, how perfectly they seemed to fit together.

Her hand came up to rest against his cheek, the gentle pressure guiding him closer. The world outside this moment — the crackling fire, the raging storm — faded to insignificance. There was only Kimberley, the softness of her lips, the subtle taste of coffee, and the promise of all that might come next.

When they finally parted, just far enough to draw breath, Scott kept his eyes closed for an extra heartbeat, committing every detail to memory. When he opened them, he found her watching him with a tender expression that made his chest ache with unexpected happiness.

"Worth the wait?" She whispered the words, her voice slightly breathless.

"Worth every second." He brushed his thumb across her cheek. "Though I'm kicking myself for not saying something years ago."

She shook her head, the movement slight. "Perhaps we weren't ready then. Perhaps this is when it was meant to be."

And as he drew her close again, their lips meeting with more confidence this time, he felt profound gratitude for second chances and the courage it had taken them to reach across the space between.

He didn't know how much time passed, but eventually he managed to put a slight distance between them. He rested his forehead on hers, their lips still so close it took all his willpower not to close the gap. "I should make up the spare room for you." His voice was hoarse, rough. "I don't have many people stay overnight."

No matter how much he wanted to take things further, he also knew they needed to take this slowly. He'd given her refuge for the night and assured her she'd be safe. He intended to honour that. There was time to court her in the old-fashioned way before they took the next step.

He felt her nod in response. "I'll help." Her voice held the same bittersweet regret he felt.

It was almost a physical wrench to tear himself out of her arms and stand. "I'll grab the sheets. The stove heats my hot water, so you're welcome to have a shower. I'll find you an old T-shirt to sleep in."

She stood and stepped into his arms again. She didn't continue the kiss but instead wrapped her arms around his waist and dropped her head to his chest. Trusting, vulnerable, loving. He could feel her heart beating against his, a rhythm that seemed to promise this was only the beginning.

He wrapped his arms around her, and they stood holding each other for long minutes, swaying slightly in the firelight, neither wanting to let go. Outside, the rain lashed against the windows and the wind howled around the eaves. But whatever destruction the storm caused outside, tonight they'd begun something precious.

Something worth protecting, worth nurturing.

Something worth the wait.

Chapter Ten

The next morning, Kimberley cleaned her teeth with Scott's spare toothbrush and finger-combed her hair. The power was still out, the bathroom's gloom making it difficult to see herself properly in the mirror.

Despite the storm raging outside, she'd slept well last night. The hot water bottle Scott had tucked into her bed kept her feet toasty warm all night despite the house cooling as the fires died down. Thoughts of him had also kept her warm throughout the night, thoughts of their magical kiss and the promise of what was to come.

The rain still sounded heavy outside but not as torrential as before. Hopefully it had eased enough that she could get home and then drive to Sydney. But first, breakfast. The aroma of bacon and eggs had been filling the house for the last few minutes, making her stomach growl.

A sharp rap at the back door cut through the rain on the roof. She heard Scott's footsteps cross the worn floorboards of the kitchen, then the creak of the door.

Easing the bathroom door open, she poked her head out so she could hear who it was. She wasn't about to waltz into the kitchen and let the whole town know she'd stayed over, no matter how platonic it had been.

"Hey, Gilly!" Kimberley recognised Shawn's voice. With his strength and size, he was a valuable SES crew member at times of emergency. "Thought I'd let you know that the road back into town is clear — for now. We've sorted out those trees that were blocking it. Water's creeping up to the bridge supports, but she's okay for now. Take it easy and keep an eye on it if you're heading that way. And Roman said we can use your help as soon as you can get in. There's a list of jobs as long as your arm."

Scott's quieter voice rumbled in response, but she couldn't make out the words from where she stood.

"Hey, is that Kimberley Ward's car I see there?" Shawn's voice lifted with undisguised curiosity. Her cheeks heated, imagining the smirk on his face. She inched along the hallway to hear better.

Scott cleared his throat. "She was working on the float for the town parade … got caught in the storm before she could leave. All completely above board, mate."

"Yeah, sure, Gilly." Shawn barked out a laugh. "I'll believe you. Thousands wouldn't."

Waves of heat rolled through Kimberley's body at the rumours that Shawn would spread. What would people think?

She shrugged. Oh well, let them think what they liked. The gossip mill in town ran on far less fuel than an unexpected sleepover.

Besides, while nothing scandalous had happened last night, something significant had shifted between them. After months of drawing closer, they'd finally acknowledged what had blossomed between them.

She now had a … a what? A boyfriend? Partner? What on earth did they call it at this age? And did it really matter? Whatever she called him, she couldn't wait to see where it led.

The door closed, Scott's footsteps crossed the kitchen floor, followed by the rattle of plates. Kimberley hesitated in the hallway, suddenly aware of her rumpled clothes from yesterday and her sleep creased face. She smoothed her hands down her sides, inhaling deeply before stepping into the kitchen.

Scott looked up and smiled at her as he lifted the bacon and eggs from the frypan onto a plate. "He's gone. It's safe to come out now." His eyes were warm, twinkling with mischief.

"I didn't want to give him any more fuel for the fire." She crossed to stand next to him, fiddling with the neckline of her shirt. Was last night's acknowledgement of what had been building between them still real in the harsh light of morning?

Scott rolled his eyes, covering the plate with foil and sliding it into the warming oven. "I don't think he needs any more. He's drawn his own conclusions." He reached out and caught her hands in his. "Are you okay with that, or do you want me to have a word with him? Try to set him straight again?"

At his touch, her shoulders relaxed a fraction. She held his gaze, searching for confirmation that they weren't retreating from last night's courage. His eyes dropped to her lips and lingered. They swayed closer, his head lowering toward hers.

"I'm okay with that. It might be a nice change to have a reputation." She murmured the words almost against his lips.

"Happy to help." He closed the small gap, brushing his lips against hers, his beard tickling her chin. Already his kiss felt familiar, the gesture natural. "Did you sleep well?"

"Surprisingly, I did. I think the rain lulled me to sleep." She glanced out of the window at the deluge. "Is it forecast to ease anytime soon?"

"It's eased a bit from last night. Hopefully, it will continue to ease through the morning. I suggest you stay and eat breakfast before you head off. I only need to throw some bread in the pan to toast and fix the coffee."

"Thank you. It smells delicious." She dropped her head to his chest. "I wish I didn't have to go."

"I wish you didn't have to go as well." He linked his arms around her waist and pulled her close. "But I know you need to go to the awards night and have your moment in the spotlight so everyone can see how amazing you are."

"I wish you could come. But it's probably too late to organise."

"That's okay. It's not really my scene. Anyway, as Shawn reminded me, I've got a lot of cleanup to do, so it's time to pull the overalls on and get to work. After we've both eaten, of course."

She stepped away from his embrace, immediately missing his touch. "How can I help?"

"Would you mind setting the table?" He pointed toward a drawer of the cabinets. "Cutlery is in there. Sauce and tomato relish in the fridge. The relish is homemade — not by me, by one of the CWA ladies."

She set out the cutlery and condiments on the kitchen table while Scott toasted bread and made coffee. Once that was done, she collected her bag from the bedroom and slung it over the back of a kitchen chair.

Rather than hover in the space, she took a seat and watched him move around the room. Hopefully, this would be the first of many breakfasts they shared in this space.

Steam rose from the plates as he placed them on the table and slid onto the seat opposite her. "I hope you like it."

She reached for the tomato relish. "I'm sure I will. Thank you. I owe you several meals now."

He gazed at her intently, his eyes dark. "As soon as you're back from Sydney, I want to romance you properly. Dates, flowers, movies ... the whole thing. I want to do it right."

Her stomach swooped, butterflies setting flight. "I'd like that."

They fell into a comfortable rhythm of eating and talking, though Kimberley noticed they spent more time staring into each other's eyes than paying attention to their food. When their hands weren't occupied, they found each other across the table, fingers intertwining as naturally as if they'd been doing this for years. She felt giddy, like a teenager rather than a woman in her prime.

The rain slowed to a gentle patter, the sky lightening slightly. Reluctantly, she picked up her plate and stood. "I probably should go while I have the chance. Do you want me to help with the dishes?"

Scott shook his head. "No, that's fine. I'll leave them until later." He stood and took her plate from her, stacking it on his. "Are you heading straight for Sydney?"

"Pretty much. Assuming Tibbles hasn't completely destroyed the house in his disgust at me not being home last night and missing a meal. I need to pack and drop the key into my neighbour's house, but that won't take long."

He opened his arms, and she stepped naturally into his embrace. "I hope the road to Sydney is okay. I don't know how widespread the storm was."

"There was nothing on the forecast for Sydney when I looked yesterday. I couldn't get a mobile signal this morning, so I'll have to cross my fingers."

His lips brushed her forehead. "Could you send me a text when you get there? Hopefully, the mobile towers will be back by this afternoon."

She buried her head in his shoulder, breathing in the scent of him — soap, coffee and something uniquely Scott — and squeezed him tight for one last hug to sustain her through the next few days.

"Have a fantastic time, all right? Good luck with the awards and drive safely. If the roads look dodgy, promise me you'll find somewhere to stop."

"I will." She stepped away, fighting back the prickle of tears. "I should be back Thursday to finish off the last of the float, ready for Saturday's parade."

"I'll miss you."

"I'll miss you, too. We could go to karaoke at the pub on Friday night if you like? For our first official date." She chuckled. "They're doing a special Christmas-themed karaoke — and I know how much you love Christmas carols."

Scott grimaced, but his eyes remained soft, crinkling at the corners. "Anything for you. Even butchering *Silent Night* in public."

"I'll hold you to that." She smiled, rising on tiptoes to press a kiss to his cheek, lingering a moment longer than necessary before forcing herself to step away and gather her things.

Scott stood motionless in the gravel driveway, watching Kimberley's taillights grow smaller through the curtain of drizzle that still hung in the air. His hand stayed half-raised in farewell long after her car had disappeared around the bend, as if reluctant to acknowledge she was truly gone. He shivered as the chill seeped through his jacket.

He'd felt almost boyish with happiness when he'd woken this morning, the memory of yesterday's conversations — and that kiss —

immediately flooding back. But now, watching her drive away toward Sydney, toward a glamorous awards ceremony and theatre outings in a world so far removed from Bindarra Creek, the old doubts began their subtle whisper.

What would a woman like her want with an old country boy like you?

He ran his hand through his wet hair and pushed the thoughts away. He wouldn't let those doubts take root, not today. Instead, he deliberately focused on the way she'd looked sitting at his kitchen table this morning, somehow fitting perfectly into the space that had been empty for so long.

Scott couldn't quite believe that Kimberley returned his feelings. Had agreed to go out with him. Had kissed him with a warmth that made his pulse spike.

A gust of wind blew a fresh spatter of raindrops against his face, finally breaking him out of his trance. The sky hung low and leaden, the colour of wet slate, promising more rain to come. He turned back toward the house, boots squelching across the sodden yard.

Inside, he quickly tidied up the kitchen, rinsing the plates and stacking them in the dishwasher for when the power came back on. He changed into his SES overalls and packed a small overnight bag. He wasn't taking chances with the rising waters near the bridge. If he got cut off from home, at least he'd have a change of underwear.

He lifted the bag and headed outside to his work truck. After throwing the bag on the seat, he made a quick check of his property. From what he could see from a quick walk around the outside, both of his sheds and the house had escaped damage. The old gum tree at the corner nearest the road had lost a large limb which lay half across the fence line. In the paddock beyond his boundary, sheets of corrugated iron, torn from someone's shed, lay crumpled on the ground. Nothing that couldn't wait.

As he navigated the familiar route into town, the storm's impact became increasingly obvious. Ditches alongside the road flowed with rushing streams of water, churning with debris and mud. A massive gum that had stood for at least a century lay fallen across a front paddock, its extensive root system exposed, leaving a gaping hole in the ground where it once stood. A trampoline, twisted and broken, was caught in the fence of one of the new housing lots.

Scott slowed as he approached the bridge over Bindarra Creek. Water surged beneath it, running high and fast, lapping at the underside of the bridge's wooden supports. Not over the road yet, but too close for comfort.

He thought of Kimberley driving to Sydney and felt his stomach tighten. It would be hard to relax until he heard from her that she was safe and checked in to her hotel.

As he crossed the bridge and turned toward the SES headquarters, he could see evidence of the crew's overnight efforts. Cleared branches lay in neat piles along the street. Blue tarps covered damaged roofs on at least three buildings he could see. But for every cleaned area, there were several more needing attention. Hopefully, there'd been no serious injuries or damage.

He pulled up at headquarters and stepped outside the vehicle, shivering as he left the cab's warmth. Grabbing his gear, he dashed for the entrance, pushing in through the front doors.

Roman stood at the front of the room, his fingers tracing a path on a large map pinned to the wall. A dozen crew members lounged about in various states of alertness and exhaustion — some sprawled in chairs nursing steaming mugs, others leaning forward taking notes.

All heads turned to him as he entered the room.

"About time you got here, lazy bones." Leslie nudged him and then winked. "But I hear you've been otherwise occupied."

Shawn obviously hadn't waited to tell his mate about the juicy gossip.

Heat crawled up Scott's neck despite the chill. "Lay off. It was completely platonic. Kimberley had to stay the night because the road was closed." He was sure he'd be saying this over and over again for all the good it would do.

"Righto, guys. Back to it." Roman scrubbed his hand through his hair, weariness lining his face. "Scott, can you go with Leslie's group? We've got a roof partially off a house over near the oval. It'll need to be tarped before the rain increases again."

"Sure, no problem."

For the rest of the morning, Scott threw himself into the physical demands of the work, welcoming the distraction of aching muscles. They tarped roofs, cleared fallen trees and helped set up warning signs and barricades to stop motorists driving into floodwater. The rain alternated between gentle misting and violent downpours that rendered their rain gear almost useless, leaving them all sodden and shivering.

Throughout it all, his thoughts continually circled back to Kimberley. Had she made it home safely? Had she left for Sydney yet?

During a late afternoon lunch break, wolfing down a meat pie while huddled beneath a dripping awning outside the bakery, he checked his phone. Still no signal. The storm had obviously knocked out the local tower, cutting them off from the outside world.

He tucked it away with a sigh, surprised by the concern weighing on his chest. It had been years since he'd had someone whose safety took over his thoughts so completely. Kimberley had become so important to him, so quickly. They were still at the very start of their relationship, but already she'd carved out an essential space in his life.

Chapter Eleven

The Grand Ballroom of the Intercontinental Hotel glittered with chandeliers and the bling of Australia's publishing elite. Sitting at table seventeen, Kimberley smoothed the unfamiliar silk of her midnight blue dress against her thighs and tried to look at ease. This was as far away from Bindarra Creek as she could imagine.

All around her, conversation flowed. Everyone else at the table was partnered up with spouses or significant others. Attending these events alone had never worried her before, but tonight she desperately wanted Scott to be sitting beside her. His solid presence would help anchor her in this world that once felt so familiar but now seemed alien and hollow.

She missed him more than she thought she would — a foreign feeling given that she'd been alone, and content about her single status, for so many years. But the start of a romance with Scott left her feeling bereft, out of place as a single at a table full of couples.

Her publisher, Marion Delaney, leaned across the table. She tapped Kimberley on the shoulder with manicured fingers glittering with rings. "I'm so excited for you, my dear." Her voice was pitched to carry over the chatter but not beyond their table. "I have a good feeling about this tonight. I think you're going to take out the award."

Kimberley's stomach, already dancing with nerves, performed a complete somersault. She grimaced, trying to mask her anxiety with a stiff smile. The last thing she needed was the additional pressure of Marion's expectations. She'd been nominated twice before in her career and had perfected the art of the gracious losing smile. Tonight, she'd hoped to simply enjoy the recognition of the nomination without the disappointment that would inevitably follow.

"Let's not jinx it." She reached for her water glass, her throat suddenly parched.

"You should have more confidence in yourself." Marion leaned closer, her mouth near Kimberley's ear. "By the way, dear, what day are you leaving Sydney?"

"I'm heading home on Thursday morning." Home to Bindarra Creek. To her house, her friends, her cat. Home to Scott.

Marion clutched Kimberley's arm. "Could I persuade you to stay until Friday? I want to talk to you about an opportunity." She glanced around the room, lowering her voice even more. "Not here, obviously. But my next free spot is on Thursday. I would have booked you sooner, but it only came up today."

Curiosity flickered through Kimberley. In her twenty years of publishing with Delaney Press, Marion had never requested a special meeting. Editors normally handled the routine business via emails, with Marion swooping in only for contract signings and champagne celebrations.

Kimberley mentally rearranged her schedule. She still needed to get back to finish painting the final cutout, but that would only take an hour or so. If she left early Friday morning, she'd have time to drive back and finish before her first official date with Scott on Friday night.

Her heart thumped at the thought of appearing out in public together at the karaoke night. Although, given that Shawn had seen her car at Scott's place, the rumours were probably already swirling around Bindarra Creek. Maybe their debut wouldn't cause half the stir she feared.

"Sure, that can work." She'd have to let Scott know she'd be a day later than planned.

"Perfect. I'll have my girl call you to set the time. I think I'm free at three, but she knows my schedule far better than me." She gave a tinkling laugh, then turned back to her dinner companion, a silver-haired man Kimberley vaguely recognised as a literary agent from Melbourne.

Alone again in the crowded room, she slipped her phone out of her bag. She wasn't sure if power or mobile reception would be back up yet, but she'd send a text to make sure.

> *Something's come up. I need to stay in Sydney*

The person next to her, a bearded illustrator whose fantasy covers dominated bookstore displays, jostled her arm as he stood to leave his seat. Her thumb slipped, pressing send before she finished her thought. She accepted his mumbled apology with a distracted smile and quickly returned to her phone to complete the message.

> *Another day. I will be back early on Friday afternoon. Looking forward to our date! Start practicing Jingle Bells!*

She added a couple of random Christmas emojis and sent the message flying out into the ether. Hopefully, it would reach Scott despite the storm damage back home. Placing her phone back in her small handbag, she surveyed the room with fresh eyes.

The glittering award scene felt strangely empty. While it felt nice to dress up in the sleek dress she'd worn to countless Sydney literary events, it was a far cry from the paint-spattered jeans and shirts that were her normal outfits. She wished she was back curled up in front of Scott's fireplace, Ugg boots on and wearing track pants rather than a constricting dress and shoes that were already raising blisters on her heels.

When had her priorities shifted so dramatically? She'd move to Bindarra Creek three years ago to regroup after her divorce. In the back of her mind, she'd always had the vague plan to move back to Sydney one day. But here she was, homesick for her simpler life.

The screech of microphone feedback cut through her thoughts. The MC stepped back up to the podium, signalling the start of the next portion of the awards ceremony. Kimberley's stomach clenched. The next category was hers.

She'd barely picked at the herb-crusted lamb during the main course, but now her stomach rolled even with the small amount she'd eaten. She straightened her spine and arranged her features into a neutral mask, determined not to show her disappointment when someone else's name was called. The five other nominees in her category included two previous winners and a rising star whose debut had brought international attention. Kimberley didn't like her chances.

The MC announced the category, then introduced an elegant woman Kimberley recognised as the creative director of a major publishing house. The woman approached the podium, her silver bob gleaming under the spotlights.

"The nominees for Excellence in Children's Book Illustration are ..." As she read through the list, a slide showing the cover art for each appeared behind her. When Kimberley's watercolour illustrations for *The Really Special Ones* appeared on the screen, a ripple of appreciative murmurs rolled through the audience. Her chest tightened with a complex mixture of pride and anxiety.

The creative director opened the envelope with deliberate slowness, milking the moment of anticipation. She looked out into the crowd, her face breaking into a warm smile.

"And the winner is Kimberley Ward for *The Really Special Ones!*"

Kimberley's mouth dropped open in shock. For a moment, she was sure she'd misheard. The blood rushed into her ears, drowning out everything but the echo of her name, the sounds of applause fading into the background.

She glanced at Marion for confirmation that she had heard correctly. There'd be nothing more embarrassing than standing up to accept an award that she hadn't won. Marion made shooing motions with her hands, her face wreathed in a smile as she gestured toward the stage.

Kimberley rose on unsteady feet, her knees trembling. She threaded her way through the tables, the walk to the stage seeming to take both an eternity and no time at all. Three steps led up to the stage. She concentrated on putting her feet on each step carefully, praying that she wouldn't trip up on her high heels and embarrass herself.

Safely at the top, she accepted a hug from the presenter and took the small crystal trophy shaped like a paintbrush. Its weight in her hands made the moment real at last. She gave a brief wave to the crowd, unable to wipe the grin from her face. Thankfully, they didn't expect speeches for these minor categories. She wasn't sure if she could form a coherent sentence if she tried.

Light applause followed her as she made her way down the other side of the stairs. Kimberley breathed a sigh of relief when she reached ground level and navigated back to her table. She collapsed into her chair, heart racing like she'd run a marathon rather than walked across a ballroom.

Marion leaned across and patted her on the arm, her smile triumphant. "Congratulations! I told you I had a good feeling."

Kimberley's face felt flushed, a combination of excitement and lingering embarrassment at being the centre of attention. She struggled to compose herself, her hands shaking as she placed the trophy in a cleared space on the table.

Almost without thinking, she pulled out her phone to take a photo. All she wanted — needed — was to let Scott know. The desire to share this moment with him was almost physical, an ache in her chest. She framed the trophy against the backdrop of the elegant table setting and snapped the photo, quickly sending it to Scott and Jodie. Her friend had demanded she send through updates and there was no way she'd let her main cheerleader down.

Then she sat back with a wide grin that she couldn't have suppressed if she'd tried. The MC had already moved on to the next category, but Kimberley barely registered the words. She was too elated to hear much of the rest of the award ceremony, the trophy beside her plate a tangible reminder that her peers had recognised her work.

But underneath that excitement was a bittersweet longing that tempered her joy. Only two short days ago, something precious had unfolded between her and Scott. Now, surrounded by hundreds of people in a glittering ballroom, she had never felt more alone.

Scott slid open the heavy shed door to let in light, the metal track screeching in protest. While the heavy rain had reduced to sporadic showers, power was still out and, much to his frustration, so was mobile reception.

He checked his phone again. Still no service. Forty-eight hours without hearing from Kimberley felt like a week. Had she won at the awards ceremony? She was so talented that it would be a travesty if she hadn't. Although perhaps he wasn't the most objective judge.

A twinge shot through his shoulder as he reached up for the last of the cutouts to fix to the float. His muscles protested after two solid days of storm cleanup, but thankfully they were beginning to make progress through the job tickets. He was due back out for another shift this afternoon, but there was time to finish off the float before he headed out.

He placed the cutout on the workbench, the *thwack* echoing through the empty shed. It felt so hollow without her presence. Without her wry observations, her laughter, even her questionable choice in music.

The distance was almost making him question if Sunday night had really happened, or if it had all been an invention of his imagination.

As he screwed the cutout in place, he caught himself straining for the sound of tyres on gravel, hoping against hope she might surprise him by returning early. All he could hear was the patter of rain on the roof and the rattle of the door in the wind.

Sunday night played on a loop in his mind. The softness of her lips, her smile, the twinkle in her eyes. He couldn't wait to hold her in his arms again and to show the world they were a couple. Even if their first official date involved belting out a couple of out-of-tune songs in front of the town. He wouldn't say he was willing, but he would do it — for Kimberley.

Unless, of course, she'd changed her mind. What if the visit had rekindled her love for Sydney? What if right now she was reconnecting with old friends, remembering all the things small-town life couldn't offer her? The theatre, the late-night restaurants, the anonymity of city living where leaving a car parked outside a house didn't set off the rumour mill. Maybe she'd decide she didn't want to return to small town living.

The thought sat like a stone in his gut. He'd been here before — loving someone who wanted more than Bindarra Creek could offer. His ex-wife had grown up in the town, generations of her family buried in the local cemetery, and she'd still found the place suffocating. What chance did he have with Kimberley, who'd only moved here three years ago?

The screwdriver slipped, gouging a track through the plywood. He swore under his breath and set the tool down.

Get it together. She said she'd be back.

One more day to go. She should be home tomorrow, and he'd find out how she felt — one way or another.

He picked up the screwdriver again, trying to focus on finishing the float.

At least the Christmas parade would go ahead as planned, with or without his heart intact. The town had endured worse than storms. And so had he.

Chapter Twelve

T he headlights of Scott's ute swept across Kimberley's darkened house. Where was she? She'd said she'd be back on Thursday, but her driveway was still empty, the windows black. Rain pattered against his windshield as he pulled to a stop, killing the engine.

Seven o'clock. She should have been home hours ago.

He'd waited at his place until sunset, tinkering with the float decorations to keep busy, ears straining for the sound of her car pulling into the driveway. When she hadn't appeared by the time it grew dark, unease had crept in, sitting like a heavy weight on his chest. As he sat staring at her empty house, that unease turned to dread.

Scott drummed his fingers against the steering wheel, then checked his phone again. Still no service. The power had been restored to town late yesterday, but the mobile towers remained out. He peered through the rain-streaked windshield at the house, willing a light to flick on.

Nothing.

With a heavy sigh, he started the engine and headed home. She'd probably been delayed by the weather. Roads could be closed further south. Or maybe she'd decided to stay another night rather than drive in the dark during a storm.

Or maybe she'd decided not to come home at all.

"Thanks for staying an extra day and meeting with me." Marion ushered Kimberley into her office, the scent of expensive perfume trailing behind her. The expansive windows framed Sydney's skyline, all glass and steel glinting in the mid-afternoon sun. "Take a seat. Have you come down off your high after winning the award?"

She sank into the plush visitor's armchair and smiled. "It still feels pretty surreal."

Particularly since she hadn't heard from anyone back in Bindarra Creek yet. She absently twisted her bracelet, trying not to think of worst-case scenarios and focusing on the likelihood that the mobile reception was still out after the storm.

Marion settled into her chair opposite, resting her elbows on the oversize desk. She stared with an intensity that made Kimberley straighten her spine. "As I said, I've got a proposal to discuss with you." She lowered her voice conspiratorially even though there was no-one else in hearing distance. "One of our authors — I can't mention names yet until you agree — let's just say they're a very well-known children's author. They need an illustrator to work closely with them on a series of books they're writing. This is a very lucrative offer."

Kimberley's heart skipped, then raced. A flush of heat crept up her neck as she tucked a strand of hair behind her ear. "Wow, I'm flattered. What exactly do you mean when you say I need to work closely with them?"

Marion's gaze narrowed slightly, head tilting as she studied Kimberley's expression. "Well, it would mean you need to move back to Sydney while you're doing the work."

The words hung in the air between them. Kimberley's smile froze, the muscles in her face suddenly stiff. "Move back to Sydney."

"Yes." Marion nodded, drumming her manicured nails against the polished desk. The sharp tapping sound punctuated her words. "They want someone in their office. Developing ideas collaboratively. Probably for twelve months, maybe more if the series takes off." She flicked her wrist dismissively. "That shouldn't be a problem, though, with the amount of money on offer." Her nose wrinkled slightly. "I certainly can't see why you would want to stay out in the boondocks where you are. How do you even live out there without cafes and shopping centres?"

Kimberley's shoulders dropped as her enthusiasm deflated. The distant hum of traffic seventeen floors below seemed suddenly intrusive, the constant background noise of the city she once loved now grating. Even though she had been excited about visiting Sydney, and yes, had mentioned to Scott that she was looking forward to getting back to theatres and cafes, these few days had taught her something unexpected — she had no desire to move back. It was too noisy, too crowded, too frantic. She couldn't hear herself think, let alone find space to create and be inspired.

She gazed out the window at the harbour in the distance, barely visible between skyscrapers. The bright lights that had seemed so seductive not too long ago paled in comparison to the peace of Bindarra Creek. There, she felt centred, more creative. She had friends, the Cyprus Café with Thea's baklava, and even the amateur drama society put on surprisingly good shows. And Tamworth wasn't that far if she wanted something more.

And that was all without factoring Scott into the equation. Her chest tightened at the thought of him. She missed him dreadfully, even though it had only been a couple of days. Their relationship was still so new. She wasn't going to factor that into her decision. But she knew if she took this offer, any chances for things to progress would wither. Maybe it would survive as a long-distance relationship, but that was a fragile hope at best.

Marion exhaled sharply and glanced at her watch. "Well, what do you think? Will I have the lawyers draw up the contract?" Her pen was already poised over her notebook.

Kimberley shook her head and rose to her feet, smoothing down her dress. "Thank you so much for thinking of me, but I can't do it. Not if it involves moving to Sydney." The certainty in her own voice surprised her. "I'm happy with my life the way it is. If there's some way that we could work together remotely, or if they wanted to relocate to Bindarra Creek for the duration of the project, I'd be extremely happy to work with them." A smile tugged at her lips at the absurd thought of a famous author setting up shop next to the IGA. "But moving back here isn't worth it. My peace of mind isn't worth leaving behind what I've already found."

Marion blinked rapidly, her mouth falling slightly open before she collected herself. She set her pen down with deliberate slowness. "I don't know what to say. I don't know how you could turn this offer down. It could open so many doors for you."

Kimberley smiled and reached for her handbag. "One thing that life has taught me is that there are always other doors." She met Marion's bewildered gaze steadily. "Please keep me in mind for any future projects, but not in Sydney."

The door clicked softly behind her as she left, the tension in her shoulders already easing. The building's air conditioning raised goosebumps on her arms, but the warmth spreading through her chest told her she'd made exactly the right decision.

By Friday morning, Scott was frantic. The knot in his stomach had tightened with each passing hour. He hadn't slept well, tossing and turning as scenarios ran through his mind — none of them good.

Downing a coffee to wake himself up, he drove back to Kimberley's house. He pounded on her door, the hollow sound echoing through the morning stillness. Her car still wasn't in the driveway, and there was no sound from inside other than the frantic meowing of a cat.

The door to the neighbouring house creaked open, and Mary stepped onto her porch, pulling a cardigan close against the bite of the wind. "She's not home yet."

His shoulders sagged. "Have you heard from her?"

"No." She shuffled closer. "She was supposed to come back yesterday, but I guess she's been caught up in Sydney."

Another plaintive meow came from the other side of Kimberley's door.

He frowned. "Do you know if someone's been feeding her cat?"

"I have been." Mary brushed a strand of hair out of her eyes. "I'll keep doing it until she gets back." Her eyes lingered on his face a moment too long, reading something there that made her expression soften. "She gave me a key before she left."

"Thanks for that." He ran a hand over his beard. "Can you try to let me know if you find out anything? I'm about to head out towards the national park to do some more tree clearing, but any of the crew should be able to get a message to me."

She nodded and patted his arm. "I guess the rumours I heard were true. You and Kimberley then?"

Heat crept up his neck. He wasn't sure how to answer. "We're friends. I'm worried about her. She said she'd be back last night to finish off the parade float, and it doesn't seem like her to miss commitments."

The woman's face softened further. "I'll let you know if I hear anything."

"Thanks. I appreciate it." The wind cut through his overalls as he walked back to his ute. He got in and drove out toward the national park, the vehicle bouncing over potholes left by the days of heavy rain. Every few minutes, he glanced at his phone lying on the seat beside him, willing it to light up with messages. His stomach twisted painfully. Was she okay? Had there been an accident? The highway to Sydney was notorious for accidents after heavy rain.

He pulled up where he saw the rest of the crew and jumped out, slamming his door harder than necessary. The sound echoed across the clearing.

Leslie looked up from checking the equipment. "Hey, where's Kimberley? Has she left you already?"

"Rack off." Scott's jaw tightened. "She had to go to Sydney for work. She'll be back soon." He hoped. "What are we up to today?"

Roman nodded his head towards the chainsaws stacked at the back of the SES ute. "There are a few fences down — trees over them — at the other side of the paddock, further up the hill there. Grab a chainsaw and safety gear and head up. You know the drill."

Scott grabbed what he needed and threw it in the back of his ute, the tools clanging against the tray. At least here was something to occupy his mind, something concrete he could fix.

He drove up the hill, tyres struggling for grip on the sodden ground. A line of vehicles was parked near the fence line, and he pulled to a stop next to a white ute splattered with mud. The ground squelched under his boots as he jumped down. Out of habit, he grabbed his phone and tucked it into his pocket, though he'd given up hoping for service by now.

At the back of his ute, he pulled on his safety gear and hoisted the chainsaw. Just as he was about to yank the pull cord to start it, his phone vibrated against his hip. He froze, then almost dropped the chainsaw in his haste to put it down and reach for his phone.

Three messages from Kimberley.

His heart hammered against his ribs as he pulled his glove off with his teeth. He fumbled at the screen, smudging it with dirt in his hurry.

A message saying she had arrived in Sydney. A message that was supposedly a photo that couldn't be delivered. And then a stark message...

> *Something's come up. I need to stay in Sydney*

There were no more messages. That was it. No explanation. No timeframe.

His heart sank to his boots, and he slumped against the back of the truck. Was this the modern equivalent of a Dear John letter? Simply, "I'm staying."

"You all right, mate?" Grady sent him a quizzical glance as he passed by, chainsaw in hand.

Scott straightened and smiled, masking the hollow feeling spreading through his chest. "Yeah, thanks."

He tossed the phone back onto the seat of the cab and forced himself to concentrate on the job at hand. A distracted mind with a chainsaw was a recipe for disaster.

He took a deep breath and pushed all thoughts of Kimberley out of his mind. Yanking on the pull cord with more force than necessary, the chainsaw roared to life. The teeth tore through the fallen eucalyptus, sending splinters flying into the damp air. Scott welcomed the noise, the vibration, the physical effort — anything to drown out the voice telling him that history was repeating itself.

Chapter Thirteen

The traffic shuddered to a standstill again on the freeway. Kimberley let out a mild curse as she applied the brake, pulling to a stop behind a tradie's ute laden with tools. Rain spattered against the windshield in a steady rhythm, the wipers clearing the view briefly before the glass clouded again. The wet weather had slowed traffic to a crawl and caused several accidents along the route. The five-hour drive looked like it would stretch out all day.

She drummed her fingers on the steering wheel, glancing at the clock on her dashboard. Hopefully, things would improve once she got off the freeway heading north from Sydney and turned off onto the quieter country roads leading back home to Bindarra Creek. Her trip to Sydney had cemented the feeling that the small town was her home. If she had any doubts before, they were gone.

Tossing and turning alone in her hotel room last night, her meeting with Marion playing out repeatedly in her mind, she'd second-guessed her decision. Should she have turned down such a lucrative opportunity? Maybe it would have been worth it for her career to take the offer and have an extended stay in Sydney. But as sirens raced through the night on the streets outside and horns blared, she'd found herself longing for the peace and quiet of her small house in Bindarra Creek where the only disruptions at night came from possums scampering across the roof. Some things weren't worth giving up.

And it wasn't simply the town or her house that she missed. She missed Scott. Being completely cut off from him, without even phone messages to keep the connection, had felt like she was missing a limb. She ached to be back near him, to have him hold her in his arms and to lose herself in one of his amazing kisses. Who knew that the quiet, shy Scott would be such an amazing kisser?

The traffic inched forward, then stopped again. Scott hadn't replied to any of the messages she'd sent. Neither had anyone else she'd texted in town, which suggested the phones were still down. She bit her lip, worry creasing her brow. Hopefully, the area hadn't suffered too much damage. And hopefully, Scott hadn't been too worried when she hadn't returned when she'd said.

Argghh. She checked the time, frustrated with the slow drive. This would take forever. Would she still have time to finish her last cut out for the float before they went to karaoke? Her heart raced at the thought of seeing Scott again, of being enveloped in his arms, feeling his warmth against her. A few more hours and she could explain everything in person, watch his eyes light up when she told him she'd chosen Bindarra Creek — chosen him — over the tempting opportunity in Sydney. The thought of resting her head against his chest, hearing his heartbeat, feeling his fingers thread through her hair sent a wave of longing through her so intense it was almost painful.

She sipped from her water bottle, careful not to drink too much. With no way of knowing how long the traffic jam would last, she needed to ration it. If only she could teleport back home and away from this mess.

The towering stone walls of the road cuttings surrounded her, making her feel as claustrophobic as she'd felt in the city. She wasn't

keen to go back to Sydney anytime soon, and definitely not to live —
not even for a visit.

Home had called her name, and she couldn't get there fast enough.

Filthy and exhausted from another day of cleanup, Scott headed back
home via Kimberley's house. There was still no car in the driveway, no
answer when he knocked at the door. Against all hope and flying in the
face of the text message he'd received, he'd still maintained a glimmer
of hope that she would be home.

If she'd decided to leave for good, what was she going to do with all
her possessions — and her cat? Would she come home to pack them all
up? Or would she send someone to do it? Would she have the courtesy
of coming to talk to him or sneak in like a thief in the night and leave
without saying anything?

He got back in the car and headed home, his hands tight on the
steering wheel. The rain hammered against the windscreen, matching
the storm of emotions raging inside him. Why had he let himself get
his hopes up on the face of a romantic night and a few kisses? He
wouldn't have thought she was the type to lead a person on. But what
did he know? His track record with women was abysmal at best.

Obviously, she'd had a better offer in Sydney that would cause her
to leave with such little notice. What was it about Sydney that was
so appealing to people? His ex-wife couldn't wait to go there, even
though he'd thought she was happy — as happy as he was in Bindarra
Creek. But no, she'd left him with only a note for the bright lights, and
it had only taken Kimberley one trip back to do the same.

Fool me once, shame on you; fool me twice...

He pulled up at his house and headed for the front door, not even trying to protect himself from the rain. He was already soaked and frozen. Another short stint in the downpour would be meaningless. At least the house still had some residual heat.

He toed off his boots as he stood shivering in the kitchen. He'd worry about the mud he'd tracked in tomorrow. Right now, he needed a shower — a hot shower. His stomach growled. And he needed food. He opened the freezer door to check what he had that he could toss in the oven while showering, but nothing appealed. The stack of frozen pizza boxes made his heart ache as memories of the night of the storm flashed through his mind. Would he ever be able to eat frozen pizza again without thinking of her laughter, the way she'd tucked her feet under her on his couch, the kiss that had promised so much more?

He dumped his work clothes in the laundry and padded naked to the shower. The hot water was oh-so-welcome. Heat seeped into his frozen skin, and he stood motionless under it until it warmed him. And that was, at least, a small bonus in a day full of disappointments.

As he towelled off, his stomach reminded him that he hadn't decided on food. He was too exhausted to think about cooking. He'd head for the pub — it would be warm, and the thought of their delicious steak and chips made his mouth water. Plus, he could do with a beer. Between Kimberley's message and the physical work he'd undertaken all day, he thought he deserved it. Maybe more than one.

Moving quickly to the cold bedroom, he pulled on jeans and a rugby jumper, eager to get there now that he'd made up his mind.

The pub's car park was almost full when he pulled in, and he frowned. Why was it so busy? He glanced at his phone, which had remained stubbornly silent after the earlier text messages. There had obviously been a random surge of signal up on the hill, as it still declared *No service* in town.

Friday night. Worse — Friday night karaoke night — the Christmas karaoke he'd agreed to attend with Kimberley. His chest tightened. Another reminder. Another plan they'd made together that would now exist only in his imagination.

Luckily for him, there was still time to grab a meal before the karaoke part of the night started. Besides, he didn't want to drive back home now that he was so close. Not with the waft of fried onions filling the air.

He locked the car and walked into the pub. The blast of warm air hit him first, followed by the sizzle of steaks on the grill and the rich, yeasty scent of beer. Christmas tinsel glinted under the lights while a cacophony of conversation and laughter echoed off the walls. His stomach growled again, and he headed straight for the counter to order his meal, keeping his eyes fixed ahead. The last thing he needed was to run into someone who'd ask about Kimberley.

He moved across to the bar to wait for his beer. Alice filled his schooner glass from the taps, then set it down on the beer mat in front of him. "Here you go, Scott. You look like you could do with that."

He took a sip. "Sure do. Thanks." The cold beer was a momentary distraction from the hollow feeling in his chest.

"Are you ready for the parade tomorrow?" She placed a pint glass under the beer tap for another customer while waiting for his answer.

His heart sank yet again. The parade — the float that he'd worked so hard on with Kimberley, the project that had seemed like a new start for them — was now simply another chore that he had to get through. He forced a smile.

"Sure, can't wait for the kids to see our float. Kimberley's done an amazing job with the decorations."

His throat physically hurt as he said her name, his voice coming out raspy and breaking a little at the end of his sentence.

Alice gave him a curious look but didn't press him to say more. "I'll look forward to seeing it." She turned her head toward the end of the bar. "Duty calls. I'll see you later."

Dismissed, he went to find a table where he could sit alone with his beer and his meal, and wallow in his own misery.

He found a small table in the corner, partially hidden behind a Christmas tree laden with twinkling lights. The perfect spot to observe without being observed. When his steak arrived, he cut into it mechanically, barely tasting the food he'd been craving only minutes before.

Around him, the pub was filling up fast. Familiar faces from around the district filed in, greeting each other with easy familiarity. Scott hunched lower in his seat, hoping to remain invisible. He wasn't in the mood for small talk, for questions about the parade, or worse — questions about Kimberley.

The karaoke equipment in the corner sparked to life with a squeal of feedback, and the pub erupted in a mix of cheers and good-natured groans. Scott winced. He had to leave now, before the singing started and before memories of planning this night with Kimberley could take further hold.

He stood and drained his beer, surrounded by the cheerful crowd yet feeling utterly alone.

Chapter Fourteen

Kimberley was almost shaking with exhaustion by the time she pulled into Scott's driveway. Through the sheeting rain that drummed against her windscreen, her headlights shone on the shed and the empty spot where Scott's ute should be. Her heart sank, the anticipation that had kept her going throughout the long drive dissolving. He wasn't here.

The house was dark other than a single yellow light on the veranda. Had he gone on to karaoke on his own? The thought of shy Scott belting out Christmas carols on his own made her burst into giggles that bordered on hysteria. Exhaustion was making her delirious.

She pulled her car around and parked behind the shed. After the rumours she'd started when she'd stayed the night of the storm, she wasn't going to risk parking in his driveway again. Grateful that he'd given her a key to the shed, she hurried around the building and struggled with the heavy door, her cold fingers slipping against the wet metal as she pushed it open. The wind whipped at her hair, sending icy raindrops trickling down her neck.

She stepped inside and flicked the switch, blinking as the lights flickered to life with a faint buzzing sound. Her spirits lifted at the sight of the parade float. It was complete — the back crammed with the painted cutouts adorned with tinsel and baubles, Christmas lights strung around the side of the truck, SES Santa dangling from his A-frame. As she approached the truck, she could see a small space left for her and Stevie to stand next to a box filled with lolly bags, ready for them to toss out during the parade.

The only cutout that hadn't been finished was her little owlet-nightjar, Scrappy. There was a slot where she could slide it in as long as she finished it tonight. Her stomach growled loudly, the edges of her vision blurring momentarily. She pried open the paint tin with trembling hands. The burger and chips she'd devoured at Murrurundi seemed a lifetime ago.

She should finish up painting Scrappy, leave a note for Scott, and head home to bed. She checked her phone. Still no signal. But at least the power was back on in town. Spurred on by thoughts of crawling between clean sheets and heating up something in the microwave, she set to work on the cutout, the familiar strokes of her brush against wood bringing a measure of calm after the chaotic day.

Given the number of times she'd painted and sketched her creation, it didn't take long to finish. She tidied up and carefully laid the cutout on the back of the tray, the fresh paint glistening under the harsh shed lights, ready to slot in place tomorrow when it was dry.

She returned to her car and rummaged in the glove compartment, pushing aside petrol receipts and manuals, until she found a dog-eared notebook. Shielding it from the rain, she hurried back into the shed and wrote Scott a note.

Sorry, I missed you and our Christmas Carol karaoke. I was really looking forward to it. Owlet is done and in the tray. I'm heading home for a sleep. See you at the parade ground tomorrow morning.

For a moment she hesitated, chewing her lip, before adding *I missed you xxx* across the bottom.

She placed the note on the workbench with the paint tin holding it down. Given how meticulously he kept his bench, he'd be sure to see something out of place when he entered tomorrow morning.

Her throat tightened with disappointment that she had missed him. The promise of his strong arms around her and the memory of his kisses had been her beacon during the white-knuckled drive home on winding country roads slick with rain.

But at least she'd see him tomorrow. That thought warmed her as she dashed back to her car through the relentless downpour, the icy rain washing away her tears of disappointment and exhaustion.

Blast. Scott peered blearily at his watch. Morning already and he'd slept in. He had to have the truck outside Fred's garage in thirty minutes, ready for the start of the parade.

He took the world's quickest shower and reluctantly pulled on the Santa outfit top. At least since he'd be driving the truck, he could get away with wearing his normal jeans. And he'd be ripping the Santa top off as soon as he possibly could.

Stifling a yawn, he laced up his shoes. He'd tossed and turned for hours last night after he'd come back from the pub, haunted by memories of Kimberley. The way she threw her head back when she laughed and her whole face lit up. The feel of her hand in his. The way she'd looked so right, curled up in the lounge chair by the fireplace.

He cast a regretful look at the coffee maker as he rushed through the kitchen, collecting his keys from where he'd thrown them on the table. He'd have to get a coffee at the show grounds when the parade finished, along with something for breakfast. Luckily, the parade route wasn't very long, given that the town itself was quite small. At least he'd be able to feed his growling stomach sooner rather than later.

He left the house and jogged to the truck, his feet crunching on the frosty grass, shivering in the cold morning air. At least the rain had stopped. Obviously, even the weather obeyed Edwina.

One eye on the clock, the other on the roads, he drove as fast as he dared into town. Fog lingered in the hollows, but otherwise, the roads were clear.

As he crossed the bridge over the Akuna River, he glanced out of the window. The river was still swollen, the water brown and dirty, with debris still being swept along by the current. He turned right down River Road to take the back streets to Fred's garage to avoid any road closures along the parade route. A few minutes later, pulled up behind the other parade vehicles, their festive decorations a blur of tinsel and colour that did nothing to lift his mood.

"We were about to send out a search party." Roy appeared at the window and slapped his hand on the side of the truck, the sound jarring against Scott's raw nerves. "Looks good, though. You and the girlie did a good job."

Not that the girlie wanted to be here to see it. Scott felt a surge of bitterness rise in him as he hopped out of the cab, his boots landing in a puddle. The float they'd created together — every animal cutout, every strand of tinsel — was now another reminder of what he'd foolishly believed they were building.

"Thanks, mate. Is Stevie here ready to go on the back?"

"Yep. She's over there with young Kimberley."

Scott's head whipped round in a double take, the muscles in his neck protesting. For a moment, he was certain he'd misheard. Kimberley was here? Wasn't she supposed to be in Sydney? His eyes searched the crowd frantically, heart hammering in his chest, finally finding her and Stevie standing near the police float.

She spotted him across the distance. Her face lit up like Christmas morning, and she waved with an enthusiasm that made no sense, given her text. She pulled on Stevie's arm and hurried towards the truck, her elf costume complete with jingling bells announcing her approach.

Scott stood frozen, unable to reconcile the smiling woman before him with the one who had messaged about staying in Sydney. His mind raced through possibilities — had she changed her mind? Was this a brief return before leaving for good? The questions crowded his thoughts.

He gazed at Kimberley in her elf outfit, the gaudy red and green ensemble somehow making her more beautiful than ever. It was a physical impossibility for him to tear his eyes from her, not caring who saw them or what rumours would spread through the town before the parade had reached the showground.

She moved toward him as if she was going to give him a kiss, her eyes soft with something like longing, then pulled back at the last moment and squeezed his arm instead. Even through his ridiculous Santa outfit, her touch sent warmth racing up his arm.

"I missed you." Her words were soft but went straight to his heart, nestling there like embers threatening to rekindle what he'd spent all night trying to extinguish.

"What are you doing here?" The question came out harsher than he'd intended, confusion making his voice rough.

She shot him a puzzled look, her brow furrowing. "Um, I live here. I'm going on the parade float, remember?"

"You said you were staying in Sydney." He couldn't keep the accusation from his tone, the hurt of the past twenty-four hours bleeding into each word.

Her frown deepened. She opened her mouth to reply, but the rumble of engines starting cut her off. Standing on tiptoe, she put her mouth close to his ear. "Looks like it's time to go. I'll talk to you at the other end."

She squeezed his arm again, her fingers lingering a moment longer than necessary, and hurried around to the back of the truck. He watched her, noticing how the morning light caught in her hair as she hoisted herself up to sit on the tray. She wriggled backwards until she could stand, taking her position near the box of lollies.

Scott's heart thudded painfully against his ribs. His mind was in a whirl of confusion, hope warring with his self-preservation instinct. She acted as if nothing was wrong, as if she hadn't sent a text that had shattered his world less than twenty-four hours ago. What was happening? Had he imagined the whole thing? The possibility that he might have misunderstood made him feel slightly nauseated.

A nudge from Roy, sharp and impatient, made him jump into the truck and start the engine. The familiar rumble beneath him did nothing to steady his nerves. As short as it was, this parade was going to take forever — trapped in the cab while Kimberley stood behind him, so close yet completely out of reach, with unanswered questions hanging between them.

Chapter Fifteen

It was hard not to be cheered by the sight of the children's faces lining the parade ground. Kimberley couldn't stop grinning as she tossed out bags of lollies into eager hands, the children's delighted squeals cutting through the crisp morning air.

It wasn't until they'd turned onto the lane that led to the showground that she had a break. Her fingers were numb from the cold despite her gloves, and her breath puffed white in front of her face.

She tapped Stevie on the shoulder. "Thanks for helping out today."

"It was my pleasure," Stevie gestured at her own elf outfit. "When I put this on this morning, Luke couldn't take his eyes off me."

Kimberley laughed, then sobered. "Did anything happen while I was away? Scott seemed surprised that I was here."

"Gilly?" Stevie nodded, her brow furrowing. "Now that you mention it, he was a bit weird last night. Luke and I were heading into the pub for the karaoke night, and we ran into him when he was coming out. He muttered something to me about hoping I'd be able to do the float on my own because Kimberley's moving back to Sydney." She shrugged. "It was noisy, so I thought I misheard. He didn't look happy though."

Kimberley's heart sank, her body shaking with a chill that had nothing to do with the wintry day. Was it simply that she had been a day late coming back? Or had he misunderstood her messages? She thought back to the accidental message she'd sent at the awards dinner when she'd been bumped, her stomach knotting as she recalled the text that had sent before she could finish it.

If he'd received that, no wonder he was surprised to see her. Especially after the way his wife had left, with only a note. She supposed it made him more sensitive to rejection. The thought of him spending the days thinking she'd abandoned him made her chest ache. She had to convince him she was here to stay and his for as long as he wanted — preferably for a very long time.

She held on as the truck came to a halt in the car park next to a float that looked like a giant gingerbread house. The sight brought a small smile to her face as she waved to Mandy, dressed as Mrs Gingerbread.

Stevie stared at Kimberley, her normally cheery face downcast. "I hope you can sort it out — whatever's happened between the two of you. I'm not talking about the rumours from when you stayed at his place. You've both been looking so much happier since you started working on the float. And watching your body language together, I was convinced my matchmaking had worked."

"Your matchmaking?"

Stevie grinned, looking pleased with herself. "Tell me I did a good job? Tell me it worked?"

Kimberley chuckled and shook her head. "Well, it had worked before I left. Let's see if I can get things back to how they were."

Stevie sent her a teasing grin as she hopped down from the float. "Good luck." She disappeared into the crowd, leaving Kimberley alone with her thoughts.

She wriggled down more slowly, trying to hold her skirt in place. Even though she was wearing tights, she didn't want to flash any of the kids clustered around the truck, oohing and aahing over the animal cutouts.

Scott was surrounded by a sea of excited children and admiring parents — the dads mostly admiring the heritage truck rather than their float. There was no chance that she'd be able to talk to him for at least the next little while. His serious expression as he explained something to a wide-eyed little boy made her heart flutter despite her anxiety. Maybe buying him a coffee would be the first step to break the ice.

She hurried off into the showground, following her nose towards the food and coffee vans. The morning clouds were beginning to break, letting through shafts of winter sunlight that promised a clear afternoon. She pulled her coat tighter around her as a gust of wind cut through the grounds, carrying the mingled scents of coffee, hot chips, and the sugary sweetness of fairy floss.

What would she say to him when she finally got him alone? How could she explain a message she hadn't meant to send? More importantly, how could she convince him that Bindarra Creek — that he — was where her heart had finally found its home?

Scott watched Kimberley disappear into the crowds of people, wishing he could go after her. The urge to follow was almost physical, an invisible thread tugging him toward her. He wanted to take her aside and find out what was going on. Was she staying? Or was this a final goodbye before she left for good? The uncertainty gnawed at him, making it hard to focus on anything else.

But right now, he was trapped protecting his truck from the grubby little fingers of kids exclaiming over the cutouts. Scrappy in particular seemed to have a large following, the little creature drawing children like a magnet. Normally he loved seeing kids so enthusiastic about things, their wide-eyed wonder making all the hard work worthwhile. All he wanted was for them to go away so he could follow Kimberley and sort out the mess of confusion in his head.

Long minutes crawled by, each second stretching his patience thinner. Finally, the children disappeared, called away by parents and lured by the thought of carnival games on offer. He locked the truck and set off to find Kimberley, his heart racing like he was eighteen again.

He entered the showground, searching desperately for the flash of green and red of her outfit among the sea of festive colours. At any other time, an elf outfit would be easy to spot. But at Bindarra Creek's Christmas in July, there were more elf costumes than he'd ever seen in one place before. One thing about this town — they certainly threw themselves into the spirit of the event.

The smell of frying onions tantalised his taste buds, and his stomach growled, reminding him that he'd missed breakfast in his rush to get the float to the parade on time. But right now, finding Kimberley was his biggest priority.

He finally spotted her turning away from the counter of the coffee van, two coffees in hand. His breath caught as her face lit up with that smile that seemed reserved just for him, the one that reached her eyes and made them crinkle at the corners. She headed towards him, weaving through the crowd with purpose, never taking her eyes off his.

She handed him a coffee and took a sip of her own, looking up at him through her lashes. "I thought you might want this, even though it's not as good as yours."

He took a sip. The bitter brew hit his taste buds, and the caffeine sparked through his nervous system bringing his tired mind back to life. "Thanks."

There was silence as they gazed into each other eyes, everything he wanted to say caught in his throat. The screams of kids, the barking of dogs, and the laughter of people having a good time faded into the background until all he could hear was the pounding of his own heart. Crowds swirled around them like they were standing in the eye of a storm. When a toddler on a scooter almost ran into Kimberley, Scott took her arm, the touch sending warmth up through his fingertips.

"Can we go somewhere quieter and talk?" His voice sounded hoarse even to his own ears.

Kimberley looked around with a wry smile, her expression a mixture of amusement and nerves. "Will we find anywhere quieter?" She laughed, the sound washing over him. "But yes, please."

Scott looked around desperately and spotted a quiet corner near Meg Moonie's kissing booth, partially sheltered from curious eyes. "Follow me."

He strode past the line of people waiting to have their fortunes told by Edwina, nodding distractedly at familiar faces, and pulled her into the quiet alcove next to the kissing booth. The scent of pine needles from the decorations mingled with Kimberley's perfume, creating a heady combination that made his head swim.

He gazed at her, letting the misery of the past few days show in his eyes. "I thought you left. I got a text message saying you were staying in Sydney."

Holding his breath, he waited for her to confirm whether that was true, whether she was about to say her goodbyes, pack her car, and disappear from his life, leaving nothing but emptiness behind.

She frowned, confusion creasing her forehead. "Didn't my other messages come through explaining it?"

He shook his head, hope beginning to flicker cautiously to life. "That was the last one I got. I happened to be up on the hill with a burst of signal."

"I'm sorry. I sent a half message by accident. The full message was that I had to stay for another day. My publisher wanted to talk to me. But I'm not moving to Sydney. I'm not going anywhere. I'm not leaving Bindarra Creek."

She took his coffee from his hand and placed them both on the ground at their feet, stepping close and wrapping her arms around him. All the doubts that had been tormenting him dissolved. He buried his face in her hair, breathing in the scent that had become so familiar, so necessary to him in such a short time.

Having her in his arms felt like home — not the empty house he returned to each night, but the concept of home he'd always yearned for. They stood in silence, holding each other tight, savouring the sensation of simply being together until the tension rose between them, electric and undeniable.

He lifted her chin with his finger so that she gazed up at him, her eyes reflecting the same longing he felt. "I missed you. Every day you were gone felt like an eternity. I missed seeing you. I missed reading your messages. I missed holding you."

Her smile grew wide across her face, happiness creating an inner glow. A gust of wind blew rubbish across the ground at their feet, rustling the paper decorations around them. He tucked back a stray strand of hair that whipped across her eyes, his fingers lingering against her cheek. His heart pounded so loudly he would be surprised if she couldn't hear it. "I know we haven't even gone on a date yet. But I'm really falling for you, Kimberley Ward."

Her eyes lit up. "Right back at you. I missed you every minute of the day. I wanted you beside me at the awards dinner. I missed not being able to talk to you. Every hour I would think of you and go to send you a message. In fact, when the phones do come back, you'll probably be inundated with all the messages I sent you."

She smiled, a blush colouring her cheeks. "In other words, yes, I'm falling for you too, Scott."

"The awards ceremony. How did you go?"

She waved her hand, embarrassment and pleasure dancing across her face. "I won."

He cheered, pride swelling in his chest as if her accomplishment was his own. "Congratulations. How was it?"

"I'll tell you the full story later." Her eyes dropped to his lips in a way that made his pulse quicken. "Right now, I want you to kiss me."

"Well, I'd hate to let you down." Still smiling, he lowered his face, his lips claiming hers, heart pounding with a happiness he never thought he would see again.

A catcall broke their embrace. Meg's Aunt Phyllis peered around the corner at them, her face creased in a knowing smile. "Hey, this is my kissing booth." She rattled the collection bucket in their direction. "That'll be a gold coin donation thank you, for using my spot for your own kisses."

Scott laughed, the sound coming easily now that the weight had lifted from his chest. He reached into his pocket for a gold coin and tossed it into the bucket with a satisfying clink. He took Kimberley by the hand, marvelling at how perfectly her fingers laced through his. "I don't think we're going to get a quiet moment anytime soon, so what do you say we explore what's on offer?"

She squeezed his hand and rested her hand on his shoulder. The gesture of familiarity felt both new and as if they'd been doing it forever. "Since it's brought the two of us together, we probably should."

He dropped another kiss on her lips, ignoring Phyllis's theatrical shake of the donation bucket, then smiled. "Let's go."

As they walked back into the festive chaos of the showground, hand in hand, Scott marvelled at the turn his life had taken. After all these years, he never expected that Christmas would bring him a second chance of happiness.

A second chance of love.

Thank you for reading Second Chance Christmas! I hope you've enjoyed Kimberley and Scott's story.

I appreciate any reviews to help more readers see my stories.

If you enjoyed this book, you'll love my FREE short novella that you can download here: www.kerriepaterson.com/newsletter

About the Multi-Author Bindarra Creek Christmas in July Romance Series

Welcome to Bindarra Creek, a struggling country town where people work hard and love deeply. Set in the picturesque tablelands of New England, Australia, Bindarra Creek is a fictional, rural community full of romance, intrigue, adventure, drama and suspense.

This latest series, **Bindarra Creek Christmas in July romances**, is the seventh multi-best-selling author 'series' set in the fictional small town of Bindarra Creek. The books can be read in any order and each book features a stand-alone romance.

Hidden Dreams – Suzanne Gilchrist

Cooking up Christmas – Susanne Bellamy

Hearts in Harmony – Annie Seaton

It Might be You – Juanita Kees

Second Chance Christmas – Kerrie Paterson

A Winter's Promise – Rhonda Forrest

About That Dance - Linda Charles

The other series are:

Bindarra Creek Small Town Christmas – released 1st December 2023

The Glitter or The Gold – Suzanne Gilchrist

Christmas at the Cyprus Café – Susanne Bellamy

A Place to Belong – Annie Seaton

A Magical Summer - Rhonda Forrest

Destined to Stay – Kerrie Paterson

Home for Christmas – Lauren K McKellar

The Christmas Surprise – Linda Charles

The Gift of Bindarra Creek – Lindsay Douglas

A Bindarra Creek Christmas Romance 2022

The Mistletoe Wish – Suzanne Gilchrist

The Christmas Jinx – Susanne Bellamy

The Grinch of Bindarra Creek – Lindsay Douglas

Christmas at Forrest Glen - Rhonda Forrest

Mistletoe Magic – Erin Moira O'Hara

Mistletoe and Blue Jeans – Linda Charles

A Clever Christmas – Annie Seaton

Tangled by Tinsel – Phillipa Nefri Clark

A Cowboy for Christmas – Lauren K McKellar

A Bindarra Creek Mystery Romance

A Dangerous Secret – Suzanne Gilchrist

Beyond the Gate – Rhonda Forrest

Protecting their Destiny – Erin Moira O'Hara

Only She Knew – Linda Charles

Secrets of River Cottage – Annie Seaton

Forgotten Secrets – Susanne Bellamy

A Perfect Danger – Phillipa Nefri Clark

Bindarra Creek A Town Reborn

Take Me Home – Suzanne Gilchrist

In the Heat of the Night – Susanne Bellamy

No Looking Back - Linda Charles

Worth the Wait – Annie Seaton

With Every Breath – Lauren K. McKellar

Stealing Her Heart – Simone Angela

A Twist of Fate – Erin Moira O'Hara

Promise Me Forever – Juanita Kees

Bindarra Creek Short & Sweet

What's in a Kiss – Linda Charles

My Forever Valentine – Sandie James

Pearls and Green Beer – Susanne Bellamy

Full Circle – Annie Seaton

Date with Destiny – Erin Moira O'Hara

A Letter From the Queen – Lee Christine

Love's Sweet Challenge – Suzanne Gilchrist

The Widow Maker – Lauren K. McKellar

Out of the Blue – Noelle Clark

Bindarra Creek Romance

Bindarra Creek Makeover – Suzanne Gilchrist

Shadows of the Heart - Lee Christine

Second Chance Love - Susanne Bellamy

The CEO Mechanic - Sandie James

Reach for the Stars - Kerrie Paterson

Home to Bindarra Creek - Juanita Kees

Stolen Sanctuary - Stacey Nash

Tempting Fate - Erin Moira O'Hara

One More Day - Linda Charles

The Vine - Lauren K. McKellar

The Ghost of His Past - Simone Angela

Joanie's Dilemma - Marianne Theresa

Buckley's Chance - Noelle Clark

Full details on buy links for all books in Bindarra Creek world can be

found at:

www.bindarracreekromance.com

Also by

You may also enjoy my other books:

Emerald Bay Village Series

Smokescreens and Hedges (Book 1)

The Hope Creek Series

Letting Go (Book 1)

Chasing Dreams (Book 2)

Finding Forever (Book 3)

Bindarra Creek Romance Series (standalone books in multi-author series)

Reach for the Stars (A Bindarra Creek Romance)

Destined To Stay (Bindarra Creek Small Town Christmas Romance)

A Mindalby Outback Romance (standalone book in multi-author series)

Making Memories (A Mindalby Outback Romance #6)

Standalone

Return to Jacaranda Avenue

Elsie's Place

About the author

Kerrie Paterson writes contemporary Australian women's fiction and small-town romance –mostly with older heroes and heroines. She loves to write about women's relationships with their friends and family, as well as their romances.

Kerrie's home is a small motorhome which allows her to lead a nomadic life. This gives her plenty of opportunity to people watch, explore new horizons, and write about what she sees.

She is a member of the Romance Writers of Australia and the Hunter Romance Writers.

Reviews can help readers find books and increase a writer's visibility. I am grateful for all honest reviews. Thank you for taking the time to let others know what you think of the book.

If you'd like to connect online, you can find me at:

www.facebook.com/KerriePatersonAuthor

www.instagram.com/kerriepaterson/

www.youtube.com/@KerriePatersonAuthor

You can also sign up to my monthly newsletter for news and updates, and download a FREE novella:

www.kerriepaterson.com/newsletter

I'd love to hear from you!

In the spirit of reconciliation, I acknowledge the Traditional Custodians of country throughout Australia and their connections to land, sea and community. I pay my respect to their Elders past and present and extend that respect to all Aboriginal and Torres Strait Islander peoples today.